CUBIC**LUST**

~

by

Gavin Hardkiss

Cubic Lust
Gavin Hardkiss

Copyright © 2013 Conspiracy 3

Cover by Merkeley???

Illustrations in hair by Fernando Apodaca

Typesetting by Codruț Sebastian Făgăraș

Published in the United States by Conspiracy 3

ISBN: 978-0-9893525-0-5

ISBN: 978-0-9893525-2-9

To the Family

When the immense drugged universe explodes

In a cascade of unendurable colour

And leaves us gasping naked,

This is no more than the ecstasy of chaos:

Hold fast, with both hands, to that royal love

Which alone, as we know certainly, restores

Fragmentation into true being.

Robert Graves

~

Wake up in a pool of blood. It's soaked into the sheets of this oversized bed. Everything is blinding white. The room big, framed by 360 degree windows. Sunlight like lightning stabs through.

Concorde-sized hangover, or I am fucking dying? I gasp for air and catch my breath.

Eyes can't see much. Looks like arrows moving through splintered glass. Jagged and coming at me.

My head is a dart board. It has holes in it from years of abuse but something is different. A quick body scan for wounds finds nothing. Checking again in the mirrors above yields no answers.

No cuts. No holes. No damage. Not like the last time.

Wait a minute. As fingers slowly slide across my ribs, I feel a thorny burning sensation on my forefinger. I got a fat blister. Feels like I got burned.

Barely able to hoist myself onto an elbow before I collapse again. I notice an open elevator across the room. In it, a Rolls Royce Silver Phantom. A gleaming Valkyrie chariot.

Illuminated and glowing like a ghost. It's staring me down like it knows something.

What the hell is going on? Where am I?

Vague memories flash like fish scales. I swoop for them like a hungry owl.

Camera reflections. The bride. The harbor. Not enough to paste together.

I think in colors and shapes. Cubed synapses. Tabs. Records. Flash drives.

Shit, I'm in pain. The universe times three.

Is pain the pleasure of last night's appetite?

I spy a corsage on the floor. More like a corsage with square flowers. Reflective and organic. Wafer thin. It's like a cubic wedding boutonniere.

I'm a two hundred piece puzzle and I gotta pick up the pieces and leave now. No time to put it all together.

Stumbling towards the window. Marshmallow skyscrapers in every direction. I got penthouse vertigo and it's spinning in two directions. Crossfader is not working and meters are deep in the red.

Get dressed quickly. Passport. Check. iPhone. Check. Flash drive. Check. Grab the corsage and I'm winging it.

～

I have been hired to DJ a wedding in Hong Kong. The details are unimportant and I'm notoriously forgetful, so it doesn't surprise me that I don't know where I am. I find myself in a different city, in a different bed, every weekend. It is impossible to keep track of the details.

My agent takes care of everything. He and the client coordinate contracts, payments, hotels, and air and other transportation. I never meet the client in advance. Sometimes I don't meet them at all. I slide in to do my work, and then slide out.

I get travel itineraries sent to my phone. Boarding passes sent to my phone. Hotel confirmations sent to my phone. Where would I be without my phone?

Sometimes I don't process any details about where I'm going until I arrive at the destination and ask the person who picks me up at the airport.

"Where are we going today?"

Airport to hotel to nightclub to hotel to airport.

These are 24-hour missions. A different city every weekend. Often multiple cities. Sometimes during the week too. An unending barrage of hotels and airports and nightclubs.

As long as I have my flash drive with my music, my phone, and my passport, I can go anywhere. Headphones are good too, but I can usually borrow some. Come and go as I please. A light-traveling weekend warrior. Space age troubadour. Traveling faster than the speed of sound. Purveyor of the futurist funk.

I trade in seduction. Supply magic. Aural lubrication. Jizm for hyperspace. An antidote for the ephemeral. A dose of the unknown.

A good DJ can melt time. Drip. Then disappear. One minute you're standing in the shadows. The next moment you're dancing on the sunny side of the moon. I don't take trips to the dark side. This is a light-hearted affair. This stuff is timeless.

A good DJ can make you lose yourself. Forget who you are.

A great DJ can make you wet yourself.

~

My magic is my music and I carry it in square boxes. Used to be back-breaking prefabricated metal travel cases containing a hundred vinyl records. The best that money could buy. Each item,180 gram virgin plastic slice of heaven. 15 minutes per side. Limited release. Only for the lucky few.

But the scarcity of virgin vinyl got left in the twentieth century and in storage boxes in my garage. I skipped the CD and went straight for the flash drive. That nimble metal cubed chip that carries mp3s and other data. Smaller than my thumb. Carrying only the best zeros and ones.

Meticulously produced in the best labs around the world. Mixed in analog and digital sanctuaries. Handcrafted and chiseled in laptops and desktops. Enhanced through algorithmic tubes and valves. Promoted through the Internet to the A-listers. Circulated on private peer-to-peer networks. Downloaded onto flash drives. Transported to the DJ booth in that small change pocket in the front of jeans. Decoded by circuits and chips and catapulted onto the dance floor through mega sound systems in the same way our forefathers did it.

I'm a DJ. A musical magician. Time-traveling minstrel. Gun for hire. I set the right balance, the right mood for the right time. I know how to make people dance.

They ask me what equipment I use. Whatever. The equipment is immaterial. I use songs. Each on its own may or may not be noteworthy, but I string them together like DNA. Each time I create a different specimen. Each time a convincing argument to the power of music. Abetted by the predictability of crowd behavior. Aided by the presence of stimulants. Magnified by the explosiveness of a subtle moment free of time.

There is an elegance to the danger that I bring.

Know that silence is wilder than a scream.

Know that no one heard the Big Bang. It was utterly silent.

What does silence look like? Only Prince knows.

Know that the sound of one hand clapping fills a void. Why? Because God heard it and she began this dance. Yes. God's a girl. Don't act surprised. This is seduction.

Sometimes a lion. Sometimes a mouse.

Some ask what style I play. Whatever moves the crowd, baby. Styles come and go. Dance music is not fashion. It's the heart and soul of the party. Since the dawn of time. Give a caveman a good beat and he will boogie. Get the wild girls and the free spirits on the dance floor and make them want more. Then you have a party. The sheep will follow.

I know how to make girls dance. It's quite simple. Give them just enough to turn them on and then turn it round. And around. And around. Like a record.

~

Blackout moments.

Yes, I've been known to black out. Not always. Not too often. But some nights end in mystery. The people I meet. The friends I make. The places I go. All soon to be forgotten.

Don't be jealous. I live in the moment. I'm a true professional at holding it down for the hours that I perform, but it gets messy later. My memories are made up of stories that people tell me afterward.

Only with the aid of a never-ending supply of benevolent celestial creatures, angels, Tinkerbells, Aladdins, and some earthbound creatures too, like yoga instructors and emergency room nurses, do I usually find myself safe at the end of the night.

I'm in a hotel room. In a warm bed. There's a beautiful girl next to me. My head hurts like a dart board. It has holes in it. Sleep leaks through. And when I awake, I have eggs for breakfast in bed and shower before someone picks me up to take me to the airport. And then I do it again.

It's an adventure. Every night a different city. A different stage. A different ensemble cast. The same continuous party atmosphere. Story lines may change in translation or interpretation but I play the same role.

I'm the DJ.

~

Did you hear the news? People no longer buy music. They buy hype experiences. The music comes free with the experience. People will pay a shitload of money for that something – a special moment. Something wild and new. Enhanced altered states of seduction. A kink in the continuum.

Truth is, they don't buy records anymore. They don't buy albums. But they pay a hundred dollars for a glow in the dark dildo that happens to come with an hour long DJ mix to set the mood and amp them up for sexual adventure.

Apple killed the album. YouTube killed the single. Pandora and Spotify killed the mp3. It's carnage. Music has been relegated to some distant cloud in the vast emptiness of cyberspace.

The music industry is a failed Soviet Union state. Nobody knows what's going on. The system has collapsed. Most lawyers and execs have head for the hills. A few are bunkered down fighting over scraps. A quarter here. A quarter there. Selling lollipops is more lucrative than selling music at ninety-nine cents a song.

It's anarchy on the high seas. The pirates are the only ones making out with the booty.

The only way to make a living is to arrive in person. Flesh and blood. No different than the troubadours and jesters of the Middle Ages.

"Are you DJing or playing live?" someone asks.

"I'm here aren't I? Don't I look good in person?"

I used to sell records of the music I made, but then I stopped making music. I sold hundreds of thousands. Now, if you want a piece of me, you need to buy the experience. Cancel Twisty the Clown. You can pay me five figures to show up at your baby mama's party, live, in person, and spin records.

I'd love to play music for you and your friends. Call my agent and he'll check the calendar and set it up. You'll be glad you did.

∽

Oh, how I love women. God's gift. The Apple. The Snake. The Eve. Three disguises that win me over every time.

The Apple – juicy and ripe.

The Snake – quick and dangerous.

The Eve – demure and naked like the night emerging from the day.

I don't especially like drunk women. Especially when they talk. Or hurl themselves at you. Or try to stand straight. Or try to look you in the eye. That unfocused gaze isn't sexy.

Though sometimes you have to look through it. Squint. There's pleasure on the other side.

~

They ask me if I have any advice on how to become a DJ.

I say, "You need to know what silence sounds like."

"Really?" they question, as if I'm kidding.

I say, "Shh. Try an experiment."

Set the egg timer on your phone to a 5 minute countdown. Now close your eyes. Do it now. In silence, count down from 20 to 1. Then listen. What do you hear?

Blended sounds.

Noise.

Can you separate sounds? Foreground. Background.

Then isolate sounds.

Tune into a conversation in the crowd. Then remove the human element.

Remove the machines. The buzz of electronics. The twirl of a fan. The whiz of motors passing by.

Feel the air breathe.

Feel what it's like to be a baby. Or a plant.

Feel the air move with sound.

Now isolate the high hat in someone's rattling tonsil.

Find the baritone bass in a smoker's parlance.

Accentuate the rhythmic patterns in footsteps.

A room is a petri dish of sound. It's never silent.

Can you pitch it up? Slow it down?

Try this in a different space, once a day for five minutes. After a while you will have all the skills to be a good DJ.

You need to be able to hear the whispering spirit when everyone hears noise.

Use your ears like a chameleon uses its eyes. Then you can lean on your taste. Or borrow someone else's.

~

I'm rushing to make my connection. Taking the train between terminals at the airport. The sliding door opens and I recognize the couple seated across from me. They sat next to me on an earlier flight. Thought I'd never see them again. Somewhat surprised that I recognize them. The only words we exchanged in flight were cold. A bark at me about hogging space, about moving out of the way while I was loading overhead luggage so that she could squeeze by. She had mumbled, "There are people waiting." As if I was holding up the departure of the flight. She got irritated and tried to slide by, brushing her large implants against my back as she sloped down the aisle. Soon after, she was visibly uncomfortable realizing that she was sitting next to me. She asked her jockey/boyfriend/pimp/husband to sit between us.

I had noticed her earlier in the airport waiting at the gate for the boarding call. She seemed languid. Slightly sedated. Her body and face had the illusion of a younger woman – firm breasts, angular jaw, taught cheeks, whisked hair – but it was clear to anyone that she was not young any more.

There was an outdated manufactured look about her like a restored car. Something like an '84 Mercedes 360. A cool ride at the time but you don't see any of those on the road anymore.

Now she's going for some washed-up-Hollywood-starlette-razzamatazz, but it isn't working. It looks misplaced.

She wears elastic skin-tight pants that clearly show that the surgeon hadn't ventured below the hip line. Later tonight, she will realize that she bruised her navel on the buckle. And the imitation leopard skin coat with its fading patches wasn't faring too well in the heat.

The man with her is more her waiter than her lover. He has deep impaled eyes that do not hide the fact that he is trapped.

The flight was uneventful. I read. They stared ahead.

My parting image of them leaving their seats was the moistened stain of underarm sweat that darkened the otherwise sweatshirt-grey of her long-sleeve skin-tight shirt. Her breasts, inanimate and protruding, were misaligned headlights leading the way. Her man was moose-blinded, silenced, and frozen stiff.

Boarding the train to the baggage claim, I avert my gaze and take a seat out of reach of the blinding light of daytime.

Her doctored beauty gives her away as a sad woman. Her skin no longer a protective outer casing. Too many voluntary surgical procedures. But how gorgeous must she be feeling, attracting attention with a wild cat around her neck and distended anatomy for all to see. She must have chosen this outfit, on some level, to feel elegant and sexy.

And then God plays a joke on her.

There are four of us there to witness the sliding doors open at the next terminal, and in walks a mother and daughter dressed in leopard leotards, trailing leopard skin coats on the floor. Inadvertently, they sit themselves next to the original feline foe.

Our two new friends are made up and decked out in the kitschiest way, looking like endangered Lebanese party animals on a bender. Fluffed and dusted hairdos, tomato paste lipstick, and curry powder eye shadow. They look like they were styled by a chef.

The other witnesses and I restrain our laughter at the picture before us. As a seductive robovoice announces something about Terminal A, B, or C, three women dressed as endangered wildcats are lined up in a row, rendering each other absurd and canceling each other out. And they don't look at each other and may not have noticed the joke. But it feels good to laugh inside and I pull out my phone and take a picture as if I was at the zoo.

~

Packets of sensual pleasure everywhere I turn. Total uninhibited movement on the dance floor. Fangs flare and bite. Bacchanalian excess in the air. Two bodies collide. The type of misbehavior that warrants expulsion from true love's Eden. They're rocking the foundation of the future in favor of their carnal delights. A dancing finger casually slips from neck through nipple to the base of her rib cage without interruption. In her perception, it is a single bead of sweat dripping the length of her torso.

Two girls dance in delight of each other's beauty. A pinch of God's sweetest cinnamon in both. The fruit is poised to fall from the tree and I am hungry.

What is it that prevents me from feasting?

If freedom is born of an open heart then I must be a captive animal.

I drop a beat. A percussive flurry in a new direction. A skirt lifts. Higher and higher revealing a slender scar. Light and delicate from childhood. The scent of fields of unpicked tobacco floats past me, reverses, and then returns the other way.

I rarely pay attention to choice of clothing. I don't care about designer jeans or silly couture. I always notice what clothes reveal or hide. My eye is trained that way.

Her skirt rises further while she crosses her legs in a spinning motion, revealing a birthmark on the exposed acreage of flesh. Beauty spot.

Oh dear lady, your earrings and your jewelry are imperceptible. It's the hidden bump of a nipple ring tapping through your t-shirt that gets my attention. You wear your pearls of wisdom too tightly around your neck. Loosen up. There's no need for watches and bracelets. I love more so the midnight blue of your veins rising up your wrist.

Less jewelry tells me that you're humble. No wrist watch or cell phone tells me that you're in no rush to get home. You enjoy killing time. Murder on the dance floor.

Facial piercings like rings on tongues, lips, nose, eyebrows, chin, or cheek are conversation pieces for the unspectacular face. A face that may go unnoticed otherwise. They aim to subvert the eyes of the onlooker, triggering new dirtier thoughts. Thoughts that an immaculate face can provoke on its own.

Gotta love beautiful women who work hard on the dance floor. Those that love to dance for the pure joy of it. They show independence. They show that they know how to enjoy themselves. I love dancers. They know how to move on and off the stage. Arched backs. Head held high above isosceles chin and neck.

Both of the women dancing in front of me are dazzling beauties – tall, lean, and athletic. Each turns heads a hundred times a day. They dance close to each other and look at me as I lock them in my solid groove.

I stoke the fire. Which one will it be tonight? How does one choose?

Shall I call one D and the other G?

D has the sensitivity of a sea anemone. G is like a starfish drifting on the ocean floor. They touch each other in such contradictory ways.

D is sharp. She is the Snake. She lies in bed at night trying hard not to think. That rarely works out and, when she falls asleep, she does so with the image of the man she thinks she needs. He is a fictional character who she has never met. He does not exist, but she will keep searching for him in her dreams.

G is asleep as soon as she hits the pillow. She is effortless like Eve descending on Day.

D's fingers are like anemone tendrils. Electric but not dangerous. You can feel her tesla pulse before skin touches skin. Kisses bounce back like springs. Hugs are like fender benders. If you can get past three seconds of contact then you will be rewarded.

She is not a good lover but she knows how to be loved. If you can get it started, she will be able to step it up.

Not that G is casual, but she is more predictable in her movements. More hands-on. More likely to touch the arm of a stranger in conversation. More likely to make the first move. More likely to float.

Together they are a captivating trill. Alternating notes in a repetitive beautiful scale. One flows with the other in a natural melody.

When I finish my DJ set, both of them will accompany me to the after party. From there, one of them will return to my room where we will play a single note symphony in the dark. A blindfolded homage to Eros, son of Aphrodite, whose arrow grazed the breast of a maiden and left a scar.

~

Down the gangway to board another plane. Destination unknown. There's congestion as travelers wait to board. It gets stuffy in here.

Checking 'em out. All the sky way commuters bustling down south for some heat. Pools of young families. Sweet-smelling moms drop eyes on contact.

Does the French boy know where I've been the last 24 hours, or does he know what I'm thinking, because he's staring me down like a zoo animal.

If he could read my mind then this is what he would see.

I've already removed the frock that his mother wears and now she is naked like a cactus with prickly thorns between her legs that have withered from the heat. She feels ripe and ready down there.

Acknowledging my smiling thoughtful gaze, she smiles more at ease now that she is comfortable with my presence.

She smells like leather after a good wax.

Her eyes ask me to come closer. Naked and unashamed, my stare resting on her ass is a smile on her face. Is this what she is thinking too?

Yes, I would hope so, but realistically, no.

The gangway is clean, well shaved and humid.

The French daughter is traveling with her family to visit Mickey, maybe. It's an extended family vacation. She is sixteen tops. She shuffles her feet and looks down to straighten her knee-high skirt.

Then she lifts it. Now her skirt is above her waist.

Now she holds its fringes under her arms so that the skirt remains hoisted while she can casually remove her panties. All pink with white frills they drop.

Discarded to the side, she is bare down to her knee-highs and shoes. She is carved delicately like a strawberry.

She squats slowly until she's resting her ass and her pussy in the freshly whipped cream that garnishes a still warm-from-the-oven strawberry meringue pie. And she wiggles her backside so as to cool down on the whipped cream. Cautious not to dip too low into the heat of the pie.

No one notices this spectacle but me.

She keeps wiggling her ass as if the feeling is soothing her. The look on her face is as if she could be lazily sipping a strawberry milkshake at an American diner. A refreshing respite from a stuffy hot day outside.

And she stands up again with legs apart and white puff lining her inner thighs and drips of creamy juice rolling down the back of her knees. She closes her legs as if to seal them shut with the whipped cream and lets go of her skirt.

The gangway begins to lurch forward. She is now chuckling with her brother who is still staring at me. He looks like a nutcracker locking to break a kernel.

Her skirt, now dropped back to knee height, is a curtain behind which an orchestra tunes instruments and stagehands set props for a requiem waltz.

Her panties lay forgotten.

Now, on the plane seated across from the boy and his sister and their mom and dad, I tighten my seat belt and buckle down.

My eyes corner her legs across the aisle. The air steward pulls a wagon of liquid sugar between us. I can't ignore her buckled knees. Hairless shining little knees, with a shimmer of meringue frosting in a holding pattern, defying gravity, begging to be licked.

~

And when the bride comes undone, how can I say no?

She beckons me into a side room after dessert. Says that she left an envelope there. She takes me by the hand. "I want to get you something extra before I forget," she slurs.

I follow her down a passage off the atrium.

I tell her that she should get back to her guests, but she insists.

We're alone. She scrambles through her stuff, feeling around in a bag for a red envelope. Unable to find it, she offers a hug and puts her arms around me. It's time to walk away. But I stay. Time to play.

For a short time we go at it as if I am her new groom and this is her wedding night. Her fingernails are kneading at wallpaper. That manicure won't last through the night. Now there are lipstick traces and fingerprints on the window pane. She's using one hand to balance and the other hand is on me.

I got both hands on the waist of that wedding dress. Balancing on toes, her heels don't touch the ground. She tied the knot hours earlier but she has no strings attached. I unravel her like a shoelace. Tied with a lazy bow.

There are noises outside the door. People in the passageway, and beyond, an empty chapel with flowers littering the floor, and further still the echoes of a wedding party.

She jolts upright as if summoned back. She adjusts and, without looking at me, bolts through the door.

I follow, folding the red envelope into my pocket but not too close. Around a corner I see her speeding in those incurious wedding heels towards her brother. She will never wear those shoes again. As he's moving towards the exit, unexpectedly, she jumps on her brother's back. It's a gymnastic leap. He is startled and they collapse onto the floor. Her hair is disheveled and there is lipstick on her chin. A broken heel lies listlessly between her legs.

~

Weddings are boring. Some of the worst parties I've ever been to. People have no clue how to spend money. They'll dish out tens of thousands of dollars on linen and then rush through the celebration to end at midnight. Oh, where did the time go? What do we do now that it's over?

How many hours spent planning and preparing for a wedding? Years of anticipation. They fear the worst. Don't want to leave out any details. Don't want to leave anyone out. It's the most important day of their lives. Biggest party ever. Holy matrimony. Two souls fused as one. Witnessed by family and friends. Flights from around the world. For five hours they put on a show and then everyone goes home. Done.

Weddings are some of the best parties I've been to. A layered cake of generations forced to celebrate together. The results can be combustible. Everyone trying so hard to hide the secrets that everybody else knows. When it all explodes with champagne, confetti, and cheer, those weddings can be the most fun. It's not a memorable wedding unless some blood is spilt.

I am asked to DJ at weddings these days. The bride and groom want the music to be spectacular, yet modest, like their cake. I can do that for the right price. Though it is not cheap to hire me to play Black Eyed Peas and Beyoncé. I charge a premium for that.

We agree to the fee. Paid one week in advance to my agent. I am expensive, but not as expensive as the linen. Rich people like to spend a lot of money on useless stuff. I'll never understand why things cost more when you're rich.

I have a few simple wedding rules. Laid out in print and stipulated in the booking contract.

Rule #1: I only play music. I do not MC. Ask a friend to be the master of ceremonies. He will know how to pronounce family's names. He'll get it right. Make people laugh at inside jokes and awkward memories.

Rule #2: I choose the music. I ask the bride and groom to provide a playlist of 10 songs. I control the rest. I have a list of 99 songs that I refuse to play. I'm not an iPod. You've got to trust me on this. I'm a professional. I'll do it right for you. Make it an unforgettable experience.

I enjoy being the outsider. Everybody knows each other and I know no one. This is my favorite thing about DJing at weddings. Being admitted into the inner sanctum of a family's most personal social space.

I'm a fly on the wall. Watching. Listening. Playing.

A fly in their privileged ointment. A small irritation that will not spoil the whole.

≈

And why do sad songs make me happy
And why do I feel winter inside
Is it that spring is around the corner
Or is it that I find it hard to cry

This one is rice-paper thin. She will buckle in the wind. I'll eat her with the wrapper on.

The sticker on this one says that she is past her expiration date. I'll eat her anyway.

We play strip poker for $100. I let her win.

We're at a slave auction and for a brief moment I outbid Genghis Khan and Hugh Hefner for that one.

This one fell asleep at the wheel. Good thing we didn't crash. There will be a little more sunrise action with this shut-eye dreamgirl before I call it a night.

She is a flesh-eating Latin lover. She tattooed her name on my inner thigh with an incisor.

This one has nipples like a speedometer. They're marked in miles per hour. Her odometer has a lot of zeros. She tints her windows because she likes to hide her face. An ass like a Porsche Boxter with an aerodynamic tail that doesn't drag on the ground. She doesn't like being seen in public. She loves to ride in unmarked cars.

This one is a thief. She's odds on favorite to take my shirt even before we've undressed.

I wake up naked on a blackjack table. Across the table, she says, "Stick or Hit." I don't need to look at my cards. Double down. "Yeah, Ma'am. I'll take another."

Her lips are like sugar. Dissolve in my mouth. She lasted 27 seconds.

In a veiled compliment, cradling her in my arms, she looks up through closed eyes and says, "You are an old soul."

≈

I'm sprinting down an alleyway, not knowing where I'm going but trying to get far away. Fast. Looks like I'm in Hong Kong. Chinese characters everywhere. Little people. Bold slanted text. Stiff skyscrapers in every direction. Blocks of it hang from the haze.

Out of breath, out in the open, away from the penthouse scene, I pin myself against a brick wall. Around me is a mess of competing fictions. I try to piece it all together but it makes no sense. Gotta get in touch with my agent.

I message him but realize it's the other side of midnight in California and it will be hours until I get a response. Here it must be morning since shops are beginning to open shutters. The streets are coming alive.

Buzz of activity. Grated gates slide. Metal to metal. Aluminum bouncing off asphalt. Meaningless Chinese chatter hyphenates the brooms which swish yesterday's muck to the side.

I'm in a street with flower vendors. Row after row of hanging garlands and wreaths. If I was shopping for a wreath for a coffin, this is where I would be. A street full of vendors selling funeral wreaths.

I reach into my pocket and pull out the boutonniere that I found on the floor earlier. My finger hurts. Square flowers seem so unnatural. As a rule, Mother Nature does not use a ruler. She likes curves.

I am comparison shopping. Viewing rows of wreaths as I walk down the street. On the lookout for square flowers.

Flowers have a short life after they are picked. Three days at most fresh. If all of these wreaths will be used then a lot of people will need to die today. A wreath is an oversized full stop to the last sentence of the last chapter of someone's life.

I've yet to DJ at a funeral. Doesn't seem right, although there are some cultures that celebrate death. The passing to another world. Death/Rebirth. Sacrifice. I like to think of it like that. Transcendence.

I see something different. Reflecting. Light glimmering from a wreath hidden amongst others. I move closer.

These flowers are different. Clusters of neat poppies with delicate square petals. Strange though imperceptibly artificial. I want to ask the old maid who is fluffing flowers questions.

"Excuse me?"

She kind of grunts back.

"Where are these flowers from?"

More grunts that I don't understand. She points to my pocket.

It's an impossible situation. The language barrier. I ask again.

"What is this?"

She wants my money and I want her answer. If I give her money, she will give me flowers. I don't need flowers but the transaction will make her more agreeable. So I buy a funeral wreath.

Taking the wreath in one arm, I show the brooch to the woman with the other hand. I hunch my shoulders and make an attempt at the international upper body gesture of a query.

She mutters an inaudible word like "Chimawan."

That doesn't help much and now I'm walking through city streets with a massive funeral wreath. A bright ring of blossoming flowers.

The streets are flooding with people. All I can see is a tidal wave of black hair coming towards me. I inch my way through the cataleptic masses who are heading to work. No one pays any attention to me. I'm invisible in their anemic world.

Eventually, the street empties onto an esplanade. I see the harbor in front of me.

At the balustrade I pause. Looking out between the yachts and cargo ships through to more skyscrapers on the other side. Cubes on top of cubes. Like building blocks. I know I've been here before.

Staring down. Deep down into polluted waters through the oily film, I launch the wreath and watch it float away. The sounds of air and ground traffic wobble and flange.

Rest in love my peace. Rest in love.

I grip easy on the metal railing and breathe deep into the distance. In the havoc, there is a place I go to and I'm trying to find my way there.

～

Ever felt so sad that you feel it in the depths of your existence? A crushing sensation where nerve endings end. A deep-rooted pit in your stomach.

Me neither.

Lonely, yes. But that's an easy one to fix. There are friends everywhere. I've learned how to make them quickly and lose them faster.

Feelings are hard to come by when you cannot compute what they mean. When you've been rearranged by fate into a reboot of yourself, you get to spend a lot of time getting to know yourself.

That's why I enjoy solitude. It's real. I'm still getting to know this person every day. It's like a new relationship that doesn't get old. Really getting to know oneself, isn't that what life's about? Figuring out your frequencies so you can transmit and amplify with integrity.

I get the whole frailty of life. I learned that lesson early. We are all made of stardust. Today's a miracle. Tomorrow's a faint possibility. Chances are that it will come but I don't count on it.

Sometimes I feel like a satellite. In orbit around the Earth. Picking up signals and passing them on. I don't hold onto them long enough to care much. About the signal.

But when I play music, I tune into a frequency and it's no longer about thinking or feeling. It's about being. There is no agenda. Pure spirit breathing through me. Invisible. Omnipresent. Beaming.

If music were Eden then I am Eve. Temptress of the immaculate order. Or more like Lilith. Adam's first crush, created at the same time from dust. When Adam tried to force her to sleep with him, she flew away from Eden into the air where she fucked demons. God sent three angels after her who threatened to kill her if she refused to return to Adam. But she did refuse. And now she rules the night with bird's feet and a lyre tucked beneath her wings.

~

The past in all its glory means nothing to me. It's long gone. And my mind has a difficult time with time. Difficulty remembering. Even the most recent past. Like yesterday. Where was I yesterday?

On my phone, I check my emails. A flight itinerary from Melbourne to Hong Kong. Yes. I DJed at a small weekday club.

That was fun! A drunken urban island tea party with poolside royalty. Typically slippery. Stylishly sloppy. Deliciously distasteful. Then Cathay Pacific flew me here. I scroll for more details.

An earlier email from my agent has an attachment. I open the pdf and read the details in the contract. Booking for a wedding. May 11. I check the date. That's tonight. Accommodation at the Hilton. Two nights. Says that I should call to set up a ride. If I want, someone can show me around the city. There's a local contact phone number.

All day to kill, if I want, until someone needs me to be somewhere.

～

We live in the shadow of the electric guitar. That loud obnoxious beast. Uncut cock of the twentieth century. Ruler of the airwaves. Elvis, the Rolling Stones, the Sex Pistols, and the rest of them. I'm sick of you. Nirvana. Pearl Jam. Metallica. You may have meant something to my parents but you don't mean jack to me.

Jim Morrison, Jimi Hendrix. Janis Joplin, Sid Vicious and Kurt Cobain did not survive their dance with the devil. And we deify these humans with petty propaganda and t-shirts.

I said a blessing when the curtains closed on the twentieth century. I said I would leave that all behind. The quagmire media culture and all its pretentious labels. Avant Garde. Postmodern. Summer of Love. Rock and Fucking Roll. Futurism. Grunge. Electronic Dance Music. If it's got a label then it's already lost its heart. The bankers and profiteers are turning it inside out and shaking it down to see what lint they can find.

Put a label on this motherfucker – we party hard and make our own rules.

The twenty-first century ushered in a new template. Tabula Rasa.

I know I have to make it all up myself. Reinvent it every day. Expose my own weaknesses. Live outside their comfort zone. Get to know my own place. I am the world and the world is me and the past is irrelevant.

Throwing stones at satellites won't get you far. More debris and waste. Got to build your own space in order to live in it. Fill mine with nitrous so I can go really high and watch from above.

I sat at a pregnant piano and wrote my one-note symphony. The only song I can play from the heart. A stutter of sound that becomes a signature. A melody that is so simple that for a second or two it is a reminder. It rings bells.

A child lets go of a balloon in the park and, mesmerized, everybody watches it float into infinity.

Throw a stone at that.

Now I have a career as a DJ flying from city to city and as long as I play that song each night and make them dance. I will not disappoint.

~

The white room. What was that? Not a hotel. Some penthouse suite. Maybe she lives on the top floor. Must have seen her in the elevator going up. But I can't picture her face.

I'd like to grow strong bamboo shoots, weave them into a ladder, and visit her when she is laying down in her night gown.

I'd like to spy on us from a helicopter outside her window.

I'd like to rewind and watch the rehearsal, where everyone got their lines wrong but kept going, enjoying being in the company of each other.

Girls are like flowers. They grow with affection. They bloom when you give them attention. If I shower her with light and precious water from a golden watering can, then I can observe how she opens and appreciate how she unfolds before my eyes.

Oh, delicate poppy

Your petals taste so sweet.

Edible poppy

Bon appétit.

I wish they would allow jungles back into the cities. Bring the life back. Ferns and potted plants on every balcony. Ivy climbing every wall. A vertical garden for every family. Medicinal herbs to heal the wounded hearts battered by pollution and high-rise inertia.

Those plants need water but not too often or the roots will rot. Grow vegetables on rooftops above the malaise, closer to the sun, so you can eat fresh without taking an elevator.

~

A storm moves forward like black pestilence through the narrow gap between buildings and sky. Not far now, approaching with the swagger of a Napoleonic battalion.

Rich and fattened on the spoils of victory. Still eager and ready to conquer unsuspecting lands before it. A huge black flag in sepia. A warning sign. Rats run for cover. Birds land.

The heavens move from sea to land with the wind. A crystal blue opening lets the sun rain its own riches. A short golden strand to warm the ailing day at the harbor where I stand.

The general, unaware of my condition, redirects his battalion and closes the gap so there is no more sunlight. This will be a daytime assault on land. I must take cover.

The clouds swarm like stupid flies around a dead rat's belly, not noticing the larger, tastier whale's carcass nearby. The heavens fall on top of me.

Under an awning, outside the kitchen of an upscale Cantonese restaurant, I notice people taking pictures of themselves. A mother's sunglasses get stuck in the strands of her difficult son's hair, as she bends to pick up a paper shopping bag. He cries. Lobster eyes pop in the kettle in the kitchen behind me. Boys hug boys. Girls kiss girls. On top, their hair, hardened after the gel dried, is wet again. I wish it would rain forever.

A fat man wearing a tobacco pipe like a barrel around his waist ignores his son by his side. Kick his shins, I say.

Parents can be cruel. I will never have children.

In a vicious semicircle of periphery, every eye around me hides itself behind dark glasses. Umbrellas pop and swoosh up to address the rain. I wish I could pry loose all the screws that hold the glasses and umbrellas together and watch them collapse. See their shock when screws and plastic hit the floor and rain hits their face like murderous bullets.

Little terror compared to that in the sky where the battalion has switched combat strategies and is backing off in a sudden turn. The sun is flirting again. Pretending to be with someone else.

I wish it would rain enough to wash the ham out of that woman's sandwich and see it float like a pink plastic raft down the gutter into the harbor.

The man wearing the tobacco pipe loses his footing. Slips in a puddle. Collapses into the gutter and, with a look of anguish in his eye, is cast away. In desperation he grabs onto the pink plastic raft that is the ham. Holds on for life.

Rain ricochets off his son's too well washed hair. The son holds a pair of oars in one hand.

Chinese characters surround me. Words collect all around like dead leaves on the floor of an orchard. I wish the rain would take them all. Take them to another place where seabirds can pick and choose carefully which words woven together make the best nest. Or tent. Or net. The birds choose words like a carpenter chooses wood and nails. Words that will last a long time and will protect a fragile nest that will hold dainty eggs in the coming season. Stand the test of time.

Purpose. Family. Safety. Nothing. Mother. Darkness.

And then it begins to hail, and the storm falls hard like pointed nails reversed through a crucifixion in the sky. Tumbling. A perfect 360 degree dismount to land point-first on target. Vertical archery.

I feel this violent downpour not in the world of my five senses but deep in the catacombs of my jumbled mind. A mind that needs to be rinsed, washed, dried, pressed, dressed, and sent out to play again.

~

The girl I took home last night has seen better days. You can see it in her eyes. Even when they're closed. It's hard to tell in the dark of the club, but her eyes were bigger and brighter when she was small. They say your eyes never grow. That they stay the same size from birth. But doctors should study her to find that this is not true.

In the morning, she doesn't look sad. Just a little tired. Even after making love and letting her sleep in, she looks tired. If you ask her, indirectly, in a roundabout way, she will tell you about a love lost. Her voice silhouetted with a troubled past. Polka-dotted with regret.

If you were able to see her waiting in the morning at the corner of her street for a bus, you may be able to trace her steps backwards.

I find out a few things about her:

A slow dance with a snowman on Christmas.

A moonlit beach kiss in a foreign land.

A sleepy afternoon beneath a weeping willow tree.

An empty cradle rocking in the late afternoon glare.

I feel closer to her after she leaves.

~

So I decide to call the number. The one on the contract. But before I call, I think about an earlier observation. People taking photos at the harbor, and I now get a flashback of a moment from the day before.

After landing at the Hong Kong airport, I took a taxi to the harbor and was dropped off not far from where I am now standing. It doesn't hurt to walk around after a long flight. It's always refreshing to take in the sights of a new city.

Standing at the edge of the harbor, my attention fixes on a family group milling around nearby for a photo shoot. Like a large family portrait. There are at least fifteen of them. They are joking around. One is the bride. Skin-tight fitted wedding dress and unnecessarily high heels.

～

You come yes. Through the headlights yes.

Dropping like rain from a sky high mushroom cloud towering a mile.

The mirror ball is wider than James' Giant Peach. Hangs like an air balloon and floats around.

The fire that lights the night sky and melts plastic makes the mountains seem small and drowning.

The air is cooling down.

Black fields go by.

Somehow we lost each other.

Too far gone. Gone too far.

Now you got some glow in you. Just a trace. Enough for me to recognize.

Me. I got damaged and I'll never be that way again. Though I'll be OK when they put me back together. But I'm afraid I lost the future glowing inside of you.

I wish I could show you when I'm lonely how well you taught me. To idle my time. To dig a little closer to the spirit. Suck it up. Whisk the mask off those doldrums. That thunder cloud which obscures the light and traps the darkness. Possess the demon, skin it, and throw the useless parts away. They may be useful to wolves and hyenas but not us animals of the higher plane. We waste from extra weight. We want to float.

I'll sew that membrane into an airtight balloon. Ha ha ha. Breathe it in. Ha ha ha. Blow it out. Fill it with my hot air. With rib bones I'll fashion a basket. Tie it together with hair and tendons. Hold on tight and rise above the fury.

Elevated and emancipated, I drift in and out of this dreamscape. Accelerate to new horizons. Stop on a dime. Shift the poles of the narrative and come back home.

Inner space is the most unexplored frontier. More vast than the darkened skies beyond the clouds with their lifeless galaxies. So much unexpected and unexplained potential lies within.

When I'm not falling out of myself looking for myself, I find myself alone with myself and I'm no longer lonely.

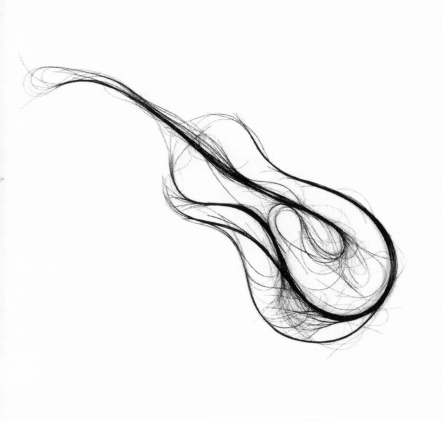

⟿

Airports are a lot nicer than they used to be. Better lighting. Better food. But it's always good to leave.

The taxi drops me at Victoria Harbor. I'm buzzing. I was at 10,000 feet a short while ago and now I'm at sea level. Reverse vertigo. Even got some sleep. Now I'm soaking in this alien surrounding. Skyscrapers everywhere. Junk boats. Gargantuan cruise liners. Old meets new. East meets West.

Tourists circulating. Businessmen come and go. Family attractions. Like a carousel, it's whizzing. Defying gravity.

I notice a wedding party in various stages of arrival/departure. Posing for photos in groups while kids jumble in and out of frame. Flower girls make the world so wonderful. They arrange.

They all got cameras. Even the photographer. He arranges groups because it would be offensive to leave anyone out. Everyone has to have a photo with everyone.

Close by, a honky tonk traveler's guitar whispers a serenade in G major. Currency collides in his hat.

Cumulus clouds scatter sun rays unpredictably. They bounce off the shiniest coils. They reflect the camera's lens.

There's a commotion. A hustle of activity. Some drop to their knees around a white heap. Seems like the veiled bride is on the ground. She might have fainted. She's whisked up and carried to an awaiting Rolls Royce.

She's dainty like her corsage. All wrapped up in white silk and satin. Freshly picked. A lover's gift. She will wilt in this heat. Direct sun is too strong for her. Someone needs to put her in water before she shrivels.

Now there's a lady standing in front of me. She looks like Yoda dressed like my granny. She says with some conviction in Queen's English, "Excuse me. I don't mean to bother you but I need your help."

I'm slow to react.

"You must come and help me. Follow me."

She takes my hand. And I go.

As we quickly walk side to side she continues, "I have something heavy for you to carry and I was hoping you would help."

We walk half a block to a parking garage.

A Rolls Royce idles, door ajar.

~

It's dark in the vehicle. Not sure why I got in.

We're moving now but I can't see where we're going. Windows are black. All I can make out is the silhouette of the old woman's face. I fumble around. There's a box. A chest. An ice-chest maybe.

In a polite pleading whisper, the woman begins:

"Please don't be frightened. You are helping us. We needed a distraction. Marriages are difficult. This one will never work. Both families want it, but the bride is not ready. Too precious. We cannot allow her to fall into this trap."

She continues:

"This marriage is a sham. A business arrangement between two families. It's crucial to maintain the status quo."

I don't know what she's talking about. I want out. Fondling around in the dark, I try to locate the door handle. But there's a part of me that's curious too. So I listen on.

She continues: "We need you. We need you to help carry the weight. Lighten the load. Take her to where she needs to be. Please take her away."

The dim light is a shade brighter now and I see her lying across from me. Petite. Listless. Covered from head to toe in the white fabric of her wedding dress. A slight silk taffeta made out of lace. She looks like a child. Gift wrapped.

Motionless I gaze. And now we're going up. I mean straight up. I feel it in my stomach. We're rising fast. And then it stops and the vehicle door opens from the outside. Gulps of hot light flood in.

I'm carrying the girl through the steel doors of the elevator into a vast room. The draft from the gap between elevator and door blows the veil, exposing eyes. I'm struck by the dodo eyes staring back at me. They are the delicate puffed eyes of an extinct bird.

Eyes lock, we step into the white room towards a large white bed. High in the sky, we find ourselves in a glass nest on top of a skyscraper.

Placing her on the down duvet, I feel like she feels like she's safe now. Our eyes have not left each other's.

And it's at this moment that something enters me and something enters into her. Something vast like the sky.

Wordless like a book with no lines. Potent like lava running deep below the surface. Familiar like a scar. Crucial.

And there's something magnetic about the way our mouths are drawn to each other. Lips are bitten. Tongues entwine and clothes are ripped as if we have help from a backstage crew. It's effortless and deliberate.

I am swallowed and coughed back up.

I reach between her legs and feel the hair, long and wet like feathers in the rain. I tangle them around my finger and pull, adjust, part, and pry open.

My fingers dial a number that has never been dialed before. A phone rings in the distance. She answers. She tells me that the front door is unlocked and I should come in, make myself comfortable and wait for her.

Her pierced clit is bursting out. It's the size of a thumb drive and I grip it. It grips me back like the fangs of Medusa's serpent. It holds me there. In its jaws. I can't withdraw. I can't move a muscle. Still staring into her eyes, white becomes red and red becomes black.

And pain is the pleasure of this love's appetite.

Gavin Hardkiss

~

First, you've got to elevate their state so they're burning with desire. You need to get them to their personal peak. Shovel dried slithers of almond wood into that fire. Build the heat. Build the glow. You've got to ease them into the now, away from the reality of their harsh urban lives, into the gorgeous present.

It's at that moment that they can let go. Start interacting with other light beings in the only time zone that matters – the present moment. When they reach that place, it feels like they've entered eternity. This is where I like to take people with my music.

Most times, the actual club night is the precursor to a wilder night ahead. Someone has to pay for my plane ticket and hotel. The club or promoter brings me into town so they can look cool and make a buck, and I make a buck too. Otherwise it's a crash landing.

After I finish my DJ set my work is ostensibly done. Nothing to do but have fun. There's usually an entourage that will insist on taking me with them on a vaudeville circus ride to the next port of call. Some kind of happening after-hours scene. A whole lot more interesting. Sometimes a little darker. Often a lot looser and weirder. Other times more personal and intimate. You never know what's next when you step on the party train and every city has its own twists and turns.

Club time is club time. Doesn't matter if it's London, New York, Moscow, or Vegas. A nightclub is a nightclub and, no matter how you dress it up, it's still pretty much the same fetid animal. There's the air conditioned coolness. The smell of spilled spirits. Dank corners. Overloaded visual stimulation. Loads of pissed people trying to impress each other. Some throw money around. Some throw their bodies around. It's a fucking circus.

But close your eyes on the shitter and hear the echoed rattling of bass through ceilings and floors, and yes, you're in a nightclub. You could be on the International Date Line with one foot in yesterday and one foot in tomorrow or in any other time zone in the world.

Some call it S.P.A.Z. Semi-permanent-autonomous-zone.

I call it S.P.E.Z. Semi-permanent-erogenous-zone.

~

I make my way to the bar. Time for the first drink of the night. There's an hour to kill before I start playing.

Sometimes all it takes to get in the mood is 1+1+1. A beer, tequila shot, and water. Sometimes it's 3+2+1. Three shots of tequila followed by two shots of tequila and then one more to wash it down.

This club is packed with rampant hormones and loose airborne pheromones. Smells like I'm at Macys. Any minute now some beautiful woman is going to ask me if I would like a sample.

They're all here to hear some famous DJ.

It's nice to get a feel for the space and the sound system from the floor. I jostle between colliding cologne and perfume to edge between bar stools to the bar counter.

Waiting my turn to be served next to a demure woman wearing dark sunglasses and smelling like roses seated next to a middle-aged inside-outside-bespeckled man.

The woman on the stool turns to me and says, "Will you give me a kiss?"

I lean in. "Sure."

And I give her a kiss on the cheek.

She says, "Are you in the music industry?"

"Yes."

"Have you worked with anyone famous?"

"Yeah. You can hear me on the radio." I lie.

"I'm a singer and …."

Her words trail off into biography as my drinks arrive. I drop a laminated drink ticket and a cash tip and turn to leave.

She leans in closer. Her hair touching mine.

"Do you like vibrators?" she asks.

"No. Do you?"

"Yes," she answers. "I've got one up my ass right now. Do you want to feel it?"

"OK."

And I reach down and slide my hand between the hard wooden stool and her soft jeans. There in her crotch I feel it. I feel the vibration. Sure enough she has a lipstick-sized vibrator protruding from her ass. It's deep in there. Almost all the way.

I grow excited in an instant as my forefinger circles the shivering ridges.

She looks at me with a delicious thrill, a string of saliva connecting her parted lips like the first loop in a seamstress's stitch.

I look at her friend with the inside-outside-glasses and he raises a palm-sized electronic gadget and hands it to me.

"Wanna take it for a ride?"

It's a remote that sets the speed of the vibrator. I toy with it for a minute. Speeding up and slowing down. Like a pitch control. Elevating and dispersing. I watch her cheeks turn flush. She clenches her jaw. Then takes a deep breath and reaches for something to hold onto.

I do it again. Building energy and then letting go.

"Early night entertainment. We were bored at home, so we came here to find Molly," he says.

I pound the shot and swig the beer, hand back the remote, and take leave with cold water in hand muttering, "Take it easy on her."

Later, the promoter's girlfriend joins us in the DJ booth with a look of sunny surprise on her face. Like someone told her a joke and she wants to share it before it is forgotten.

She tells us, "Holy shit!! There was a woman in the bathroom with jeans around her ankles wearing a thong. I could have sworn that she was cleaning a vibrator in the sink."

~

A lot of people in this world live in cold urban shit holes locked up in harsh realities. Toxic cities way up North of Cancer. Given the choice, an arm's length from the equator is where I would choose to be. And I'd roll over to the other side. Back and forth. Straddling the imaginary line.

I'd take the threat of a hurricane over a cold winter's day.

Most people don't have the choice. Most of Asia, Europe, and North America has winters cold as hell.

I have a theory that most Europeans work hard so that they can have a summer vacation. Two weeks on an island like Ibiza or elsewhere on the Mediterranean make up for a mediocre forty hour work week with wet shoes, broken umbrellas, and expensive heating bills. Those two weeks are what they look forward to all year. It's all for that.

In their cold dark cities where nothing grows, on weekends, they go to nightclubs, so that the DJ (and the drugs) can conjure up that summer feeling. That warm fuzzy good-to-be-alive buzz. For a few hours, they can make-believe it's summer right now. They get out of their heads and, for a moment, they are where they most want to be. On an island called Paradise.

I can't stand nightclubs but I've got to put up with them.

VIP rooms are the worst. People wasting their money on overpriced bottles of booze feeling they are entitled to be important enough to be my friend. Fuck off!! Leave me alone.

The DJ booth gives little protection.

At least the after party filters out the riff-raff. You'll get the best and worst staying out past dawn. The drunk amateurs fall asleep. The best and worst will keep it going and keep you laughing. And you'll end up in places that few will ever see.

You have to know somebody who knows somebody. They don't advertise this stuff online. And oh, the places you'll go!

Mansions and castles and penthouses and recording studios and dens. Basements and attics and tenements and wigwams.

Rubbing elbows with soon to be heroes. Loose limbed antics. Pants off dance offs. House music karaoke. Fun & games.

Small time criminals, hustlers, comedians, artists, and musicians. I'll take them anytime over the VIPs.

~

I'm grooving on the decks.

When you catch a groove it's like catching a wave. You can ride all night. But you've got to make good choices. What comes next is crucial otherwise the wave will crash. It's all about selections. As the DJ, it's in your hands. Make a bad one, not the end of the world. There's always the next. They come in sets. You can see them on the horizon. Sometimes you've gotta break it down so that you can build it up again.

You can't plan this shit. It makes itself up.

A real DJ shifts with the forces. Avoiding the gales and droughts. Makes it up as it goes. You can't walk in with a playlist. Might as well hire a robot. Or a guy dressed as a robot. Or not pay anyone at all.

There's a party going on here. Subtle grooves. Space on the dance floor. Space to move.

My hips slide like rumba. Mixing records. Fluid motion. And then I feel it. There's a hand on my ass. I glance over my shoulder. All I see is the bar help. A young Mexican guy. Behind him, the bartender. She's serving up drinks in a tank top. Her tips are better that way.

It's Sunday. DJ booth and bar wrap around together in a lazy maze. Like this weekend. Sometimes you've got to double back and try another route.

I'm on an island. I see the sea. Dancing bodies silhouetted in the foreground. I'm an island behind the decks.

Not much rest since the other day. Kept awake by the indigenous flora and fauna. Lots of tropical flavors. Been left breathless a few time. Wild mustangs and swift gazelles flit back and forth across the dance floor. Thick accents. Broad smiles. Everyone shines like the sun. Some engage in photosynthesis and in that way seem to slow down time.

And there it is again. A hand on my ass. I look over my shoulder. No barback this time. Only the bartender. She smirks and dips a curtsey of sorts.

I signal for a drink. That international twist of the wrist to the mouth.

She ambles over with a bottle woven in reeds. The local rum. Perfect pirate feed.

She's got tattoos like a tree has bark. They only stop for the tips of branches. Lovely limbed specimen. Genus of the cherry tree. Prunus Avium. Wiry and strong. Firmly rooted. Deciduous.

She whispers in my ear. "Put on a long record and meet me downstairs. I need your help."

She doesn't mean carrying boxes but that's what I have in mind.

Down the rickety basement stairs there is a storage room. When I get to the bottom, she's already climbing a ladder on the other side. She's heading towards a glass urn perched on the top shelf. The urn is filled with red syrupy liquid.

She hesitates in heels.

The tree climbs the ladder.

I move closer.

She moves higher.

As she moves, I notice the branch on her leg rising. It rides up her little skirt. Like a vine it wraps around her inner thigh reaching for something warm like the sun.

It spreads as she reaches for the glass container. I can see glutes and the darkness between. She beckons me closer and heaves the weight of the urn around. I grab it, careful not to spill, and place it on the ground.

"Try one," she says.

I reach inside and grab for a cherry floating on the surface. Stewing and sweetened.

As I lift my head, I find myself between her legs. Short skirt over my head like a lampshade. Cherry in my mouth.

"Let's save that one for later," she says.

And she lowers her pussy down past my forehead, my nose, and onto my lips. Like a child up a tree exploring crevices, I safely lodge the cherry inside. My tongue a spoon.

It pops into position with the stem hanging downwards. And down she comes.

Moments later, I'm back on the decks. The playback countdown reads sixty-three seconds left. Enough time to make a selection and mix in the next track.

And the beat goes on and on. It can't stop won't stop.

~

After a long DJ set, it's difficult to talk. I mean to have a conversation is so hard. So many rhythms colliding and reshaping where words don't require a response. No room for dialog. I prefer your silence.

The promoter and his friends want a piece of me but their words have no meaning. I smile and nod.

They invite me back into the VIP room.

The next DJ is on now. He has jagged edges that hide a harebrained plan which I want no part in. It's time for me to touch the ground. Come down from such mighty heights. Recalibrate.

Seated on a plush couch buzzing people all around me, a waitress shifts through and hands me a tumbler. Some local spirit with three cubes of ice and a dainty posterior.

Without looking up, I take the glass, swallow the liquid in one gulp, and catch the knotted cherry stem in my mouth.

Aged rum. Sugarcane fermented with wild yeast. Browned from stewing in charred barrels in tropical climates. A favorite of mine.

Gavin Hardkiss

～

I wake up. I'm strapped to a bed. Can't move a limb. I'm sixteen and it's the year 1998 and something happened. They don't want me to get up. They don't want me to move.

The doctor arrives with a puzzled look on his face. If he was a jigsaw, he would be missing pieces. How does he get dressed in the morning? How does he put himself together?

How many days go by? How many doctors stop by? They have so many questions. I have no answers. I have no words. I think they are used to their patients being a certain way. Maybe afraid of them. Maybe the patient is afraid. This is something different. Like being Houdini trying to find his way out of a dolphin. It's confusing. I feel OK but they're trying to figure out what's wrong.

Question marks dance around their faces like lint. Sometimes they catch a spark of light. Sometimes they twirl upside down and settle on the doctor's skin.

They come in the form of jokes.

Knock knock.

Who is there?

Lint?

Lint who?

Lint Eastwood.

I laugh out loud. They stare in shock. They can't see humor. They only understand pain. That's the raw material that they work with. They make notes on lined white pads whispering all the while. Under their breath. Inside their hushed words lurks the smell of hungry stomachs.

"Angelman Syndrome," one whispers.

"It's a peculiar dichotomy," says another.

"Acquired Savant Syndrome," says a cross-eyed neurologist.

After months, they send me to a psychiatric long-term care facility for neuro-genetic disorders. Complications from brain injury. A place called Tara. For observation. Ornamental on the outside. Stark on the inside. Nice gardens though.

And that's where I spend most of a few years. When they don't need me for therapy or observation, I float around the gardens.

Between the epileptic episodes and fainting spells, I hear shapes and see sounds. At first it's confusing and disorienting and my knees buckle. It's as if the head injury has unlocked a part of my brain that I could not access before. That no one else can get at.

Blobs that I see resolve into blocks that move like square waves. Moving shapes go through my mind and I hear music twenty-four hours a day.

In the garden I practice my slow insane walk. Head down foot shuffles. How long can I go without raising the soles of my feet from the ground? Steps are hardest. I navigate around them. It's easier going down.

I stare at clouds. Watch them bombard each other. Some are higher than others. They twist into each other and make new formations. Sometimes they don't move at all other than at the edges. They hide the sunlight in a serenade.

So many subsonic sounds. Most people ignore them. Birds call. Coins drop. Bells peal. I love the bells. Wind chimes are like sweet nectar. The weather vane on the roof has something that twinkles in the wind. It drops like mercury. I can tell when there are new arrivals because of the doorbell. An echoing tinny strike that cuts through clutter.

The jangle of keys. Clattering and jingling as they persuade doors to open. Front doors. Metal gates. Medicine cabinets.

Even the madness of the dining hall has its own metallic carefulness as food is served. Metal on metal scraping sounds punctuate clattering plates. There's a dramatic surge to the orchestration of the dining experience. I like to get there early to get good seats.

Occasionally, there's a nurse on duty who I adore. She has a lip gloss smile. She looks so official in her white nurse's outfit. She is strong but not like a soldier. Short sleeves even when it's cold. Neat with a ribbon. I mean in her hair. Blonde and wavy.

Today, moored on the bank of the garden pond, a canoe appears. She shows it to me and encourages me to get inside and row. Floating on the water is nice. I lay back and watch the sky. Mist rising off the water seems to merge with clouds.

I watch her through the mist. A solid authority with a shining lip gloss smile. Behind her the stone-walled home. Everything lined up in a row.

It becomes a pattern that I most look forward to. Things line up when she's around. We shuffle to the canoe. I drift on the pond for a while until I hear a brass bell that means it's time to come inside.

During these sojourns, I meet the swans. A family of waterfowl who I follow around. Paddling behind the mother and father and their fledglings.

On land and in the water, I join in their waddle. I'm the outsider. The ugly duckling trying to make an impression on mother swan. All her babies in tow. Me slower behind them. Shuffling feet along the water's edge. Wading in the canoe.

Swans are nature's paragons, chivalric through and through. Brave and powerful and beautiful. They usually mate for life.

The doctors and nurses think I'm nuts, but that's the idea.

At first, mother swan tries to get as far from me as possible. After a while she accepts me. The last one in the line.

The ugly one in the back that looks nothing like a swan. At least she plays along. Which works well because, over time, I'm left alone by the staff. They give me time to cruise with my adopted feathered family.

No doubt it's fun being a swan. Eat all day and look pretty. Hang out with family. Visit friends. Dip under the water when it gets hot.

They show me parts of the pond that I have not seen. It's larger than I thought. More like a little lake. With inlets and alcoves. I follow through reeds and venture to the opposite side.

From there, on the other side, for the first time, I notice a mansion. Solitary and old. Made of stone like a castle but with no turrets. Some days, I notice something curious going on inside. I can tell by the line of cars parked in the circular driveway. People coming and going. It whispers loudness. Steaming windows attenuate when opened. This only occurs on the days that the lip gloss nurse is on duty. Must be Sunday because the doctors aren't around.

So begins a Sunday ritual. Lip gloss nurse guides me to the canoe. I give an invisible ticket to no one, board ,and row towards the reeds looking for swans. She leaves me alone. Sometimes for hours.

Aiming my canoe towards the reeds, I make a line for the mansion. Muffled loudness. Laughter. Repetitive nonsense. Drowned drums like the beat in my own chest. Regular and reliable.

Sometimes there's chanting. A repetitive calling.

The simple monotony entrances me and goes on forever. Echoed between the reeds and muddy shore. It bounces back across the lake so that I can hear it from multiple directions.

I take to banking the canoe behind reeds in an alcove on the other side and exploring. Sneaking the short distance to the stone outer walls of this alluring palace. A castle. Not a castle. Maybe a mansion or country estate. I peek through the windows of the pool house. Rubbing small circles so I can see inside.

There I listen to the most enchanting sounds I've ever heard that bounce with regularity and predictability and drift and hang and hover. Sounds that lure me in. Like a mariner lured towards a shipwreck on a rocky coast. To this primitive island I go.

Through fogged up windows, I see life as I've never seen before. Life of leisure. A life of joy. An endless party. A land of pleasure. Men and women behaving badly. Enjoying themselves. Everyone at play.

There is no sense of danger. People dance and embrace in the water and all around it. Welcome to paradise.

So I commute. Every Sunday. When I can. I align the canoe with the reeds and let the siren's call pull me into this magnetic vortex.

There's a lot of dancing. Writhing. Half naked. Getting up on the one. Getting down on the two. An incessant soundtrack. Natural and artificial. Human and synthetic. Sounds of chemical reactions that heat up into an arid smoke. They congeal and bond and evaporate and float with dust in the air only to precipitate back into new forms. The rise is smooth. The fall is cushioned. Up and down.

~

Beyond the steamed-up windows I find this breathtaking world.

An indoor tropical paradise. The pool swirls like a Jacuzzi clockwise around a center island on which there is a single olive tree. Ancient with gnarled arms and fingers that go everywhere in search of spring.

Around the island friends dip and dive and socialize. Floating on inflatable penguins, crocodiles, pterodactyls, and other overgrown plastic rafts. Playfully bouncing about like immortalized deities.

Acting like children who have not a care in the world.

An inverted pirate flag hangs from the olive tree. As do bikini tops and towels.

Above the pool, hanging from the rafters, is an audacious set of trapeze swings. The strongest, leanest, and most agile girls swing and traipse with balance and acuity. Hoisting and swinging and tumbling into the water. Circus arts with a liquid net.

It's the music that keeps them going. Keeps the light-hearted experiment flowing. And it flows for hours.

Who is in charge here? Who is the captain of this ship? The man with the natty beard behind the musical devices. Driving faders from left to right and up and down to bring harmony to this outrage. Twisting knobs, he illuminates uncharted territory. Listen to the uninterrupted soliloquy that goes on for hours. There's a message in the music. Did you feel that sudden shift? He cuts an impeccable channel through the morning fog. He's such a smooth sailor.

Trust in him. He'll never take you off course. And if he does, it's for some good purpose. To check out something different. A bird of paradise. A roadside attraction. A blast from the past. A future relic. An arboreal sunrise. He'll always get you to where you want to go. Even though you can never predict where that will be. And without leaving the dance floor, it may take a few extra hours, but you arrive.

They call him Weva. He's been DJing since the dinosaurs. Some say Thomas Edison gave him his first record. He has long hair. Light on his bobbing head. Hands poised out in front like he's giving a blessing. Or mixing a giant cocktail. Circular motions. He keeps the music flowing between his fingertips.

Behind him a glorious overgrowth of cactus and other succulents. Above him, off center and to the side hangs an empty cage. Big enough to fit a child. Or a very large bird of prey. Flanking him, an array of speakers.

This is where I go from half living to being alive.

~

I can't stay long. I'd prefer to stay all day. I return often. I look forward to it all week.

And on the nth visit, I make friends with a cherub not much older than me. A teenager with a little baby fat and an eye for surprise. One day in the not too distant future she will teach me about plumping.

She spies me through the hazy window. Ignores my surprise. Invites me with a coy smile. Opening the sliding door, she takes my hand. Leads me in.

Inside now, she parades me like a pony. Then we're dancing. We haven't exchanged words. Only giggles and smiles. And it's all so familiar to me. And it feels like home.

I return each Sunday.

Sometimes I like to perch in the birdcage above Weva and watch him mix. Flipping through records. Pulling a few. Choosing the next track. Balancing the earphone on one ear. Working the pitch control between thumb and forefinger. Adjusting the equalizer. Blending the mix. Fixing it just right.

Sometimes I like to sneak around and see what antics people are up to. Drugged up sexy maneuvers are so out in the open that it seems so right. And it is.

I get my first taste of candy. It's the cherub that leads me into a side room where she takes off her t-shirt and takes control of me.

Some will spend a lifetime seeking a new whiff of that tangy fragrance of young sweat that has coalesces back into the skin and hair. Cheap shampoo with evaporated perspiration. I hold that precious scent in a petite perfume bottle locked in the deepest recesses of my heart.

And it's all so rhythmic, the way my tongue darts in and out. Marshmallows and caramel have nothing on the new flavors that I come to taste this day. The sway of her hips pulses like a shimmy. One goes back and the other one forward. Reverberating throughout both of our bodies. With momentum like this, locked in a groove with the music, we can ride all day.

Gavin Hardkiss

~

Can you tell
I'd like to smell you
Walk behind you
Catch your fragrance
Lean in close
To breathe your hair
The subtle scents
That you don't know you wear
Sit in your chair
When you're no longer there
And feel your presence
Your perfumed essence
Still floating in the air.

~

A few essential life lessons are learned.

Lesson #1 – music and sex are intertwined like vines reaching around each other in search of light and heat.

Lesson #2 – in the bedroom, let your partner work it out but always hang on longer.

Lesson #3 – it's all about your imagination when it comes to erotic foreplay. Anyone can knock one out.

I can take this to my grave.

Within these brick walls, I learn everything that I need to know. Stuff they don't teach in schools. Sins of the Bible that make life worth living.

There's nothing to be ashamed of darling. We're flesh and blood with a spark of the divine. We're a human mess. Pleasure is the pay off before we die.

I learn how to light a fire, tend it, and keep it burning. Honorable decadence. Noble sexuality. Music and the mating dance.

There's a time for trash and a time for elegance. Know which is which and know that sometimes they switch. In the blink of an eye.

A lesson on invisibility is one that is important too. You can't wear your pleasure on your sleeve. You've got to hide it in a secret pocket. Some people will rob you if it's out in the open or if you give of it too freely.

∽

So when I return to Tara after my Sunday morning jaunts around the pond, I hide the excitement of my adventures. I'm taxed and drowsy. Too much fun keeping up with the swans. Time to rest.

There is remarkable improvement, they say. Doctors are pleased with my progress. Their therapy is working. They pat my back and they pat their backs too. Then they write papers that get published in medical journals which earn them more pats on the back.

Noticing my ear for sound, my awareness of sonic cues, how my head cocks when bells ring in the distance, they introduce me to a piano in a dusty room the size of a closet. Some kind of Oliver Sacks musical therapy that one of the doctors wants to test.

With cunning, I resist at first so they are pleased when I take to it. With one finger I play Sunday melodies floating in my head. Simple repetitive nonsense.

It's the off-key piano that makes the melodies glide towards shady and suspicious. Like a high class escort working a ghetto street corner. Incongruous. Alluring.

One finger. Three black keys. The possibilities are endless. It's the repetition of something wonderfully simple that keeps me engaged.

Shoulders curled. Back hunched. Eyes closed. Ears perked. One finger dancing on the black keys. Pressing. With meaning. Until it hurts.

One melody emerges and it's perfect.

~

When the doctor first tells me that I will never be able to have children, what begins with a short gasp quickens into relief. After a spell of deep thought, it becomes apparent that this is a blessing. Some may drown in this news but I grasp and own the enormity of the gift. Like being told in a game of snakes and ladders that there is a second and third die and that the snakes go up instead of down. Everyone has to play by the old rules but I don't. This is my reversal of fortune.

The well-heeled road to adulthood is not for me. A future with kids and families and mortgages disappears. I will be flying solo. A phantom fluttering in the winds of time to any destination I choose.

In nature's own game of dice, I am rejected from the survival of the fittest contest. Stripped of all future commitments, I can do anything. Be anything.

～

I hear the Doppler pitch shift of a honk approaching. A Honda Ninja pulls up next to me. My ride has arrived at the harbor to swoop me up and show me around Hong Kong.

She asks if I'd like to see the tourist spots. I tell her half-jokingly that I'd like to visit an opium den.

She chuckles, as I lift myself onto the seat.

"I know the perfect place."

We duck and dive through some alleyways barely wide enough to fit a donkey. Not too far, we find the place. Heavy doors and heavy set security, common in worlds that separate street life from elite life, hide the opulent society that holds court in private.

Now there's a one-eyed chap not much more than five feet high lighting a pipe in front of me and I'm sucking sweet vapor.

~

When you're in the opium den and you realize that an hour ago you were in a foreign harbor in the rain and an hour from now you'll be out of your mind barely able to adjust your position on a celestial cushion, you may think that there's still time to make a fast getaway.

But you can't, because what got you here will lead you straight to where you need to go next. That's how life works. When someone takes you by the hand, you go.

It's a decadent dimly lit grotto with men of all ages curled up on velvet chaise lounges. Ornately decorated folding floor partitions create some privacy. Much more European than I would have imagined. Like a hotel for penthouse pirates and country club vagabonds.

The gentleman across from me looks like he's been in here for a hundred years. Could turn to dust if the trade winds blow wrong.

It smells like roasting hazelnuts. Warm and comforting.

I've gotten high eating medicinal poppies that a friend grew on his balcony once before. The seeds and petals made for a vibrant day.

But the sap is where it's at. And there's only one way to take it.

Opium neither burns nor converts into smoke. Rather, it is distilled into vapor through an age-old chemistry. It requires meticulousness of precision. Lamp oil. Coconut, peanut, or other. A specially designed lamp with a chimney and a properly trimmed wick.

The craft of committing the dainty spindle to heat is precise. The proper distance and downward angle of the pipe bowl over the lamp flame exact. The spinning of the tiny hole of the pipe bowl dignified. These are all necessary to facilitate the exact degree of heat required to bubble the caramel paste into vapor.

There are those who might say that opium smoking is a science. I would vouch to say that it's more a magic art of alchemy. The spirit of eternity distilled into a wisp. A secret flurry of clouded air passed down over centuries.

There's no faking this. Skills with a bong are useless here. I trust the one-eyed happy chap to take it easy on this virgin.

Gavin Hardkiss

It gets warm and cozy and I don't wanna move much. Enter the void.

Words in books and letters in words in the libraries of my mind dissolve. Like ink returning to a pen.

Enter the most precious silence in which everything and nothing makes sense. A perfect equilibrium. A silent song. Like a feather in the wind.

In his essay *Confessions of an English Opium Eater*, Thomas De Quincey says of the forbidden plant of joy: "Thou hast the keys of Paradise, O just, subtle, and mighty opium."

Stranded in a cold rainy harbor, I see how the black smoke can become a best friend. Someone to depend on. A dragon to dance with when the dancing stops.

You could live your life with this silent friend and forget everything.

~

T he poppy is the most precious flower. However, below its dainty petals hides the most powerful cauldron of sorcerer's milk. Its contribution to medicinal science is as staggering as its generosity to literature and art.

Within this sap lurks the atomic center of the most powerful sedative known to man. Used and abused through centuries by doctors and addicts alike, there are magically dangerous properties at work.

Since the Stone Age, Opium, Morphine, Heroin, Codeine, Laudanum, and Thebane have been extracted from the poppy as potent forms of pain relief. In the right doses they can bring comfort.

Both the Merck and Bayer pharmaceutical companies have made fortunes marketing variations of these drugs in nefarious ways including as cough medicine for children. They continue to conceive and sell newer preparations of the drug in the form of Oxicontin, Percocet, and others.

No drug has ever been found to match the pain killing effects of the Opioids of the poppy.

Although effectively illegal in most countries, regulated medicinal poppy production is allowed in some countries including the USA, Australia, and the UK. In a contradiction of colossal proportions, companies like Johnson & Johnson and GlaxoSmithKline own licensed poppy farms. I wouldn't be surprised if some of the molecules in the pills in your mother's medicine cabinet spent some time ripening in the sun in Afghanistan.

The poppy is a curiously romantic plant. In addition to its pain killing properties, it also has stimulatory effects.

Opium induced hallucinations were the source of inspiration for Carroll's fantasies, Keats's sensual imagery, Shelley's laments, Schiller's ballads, Chopin's serenades, Wilde's musings, and countless other treasures of Romantic literature, music, and the arts.

The French artist Jean Cocteau writes, "Opium is the only vegetable substance that communicates the vegetable state to us."

What he means by that, I believe, is that opium unfolds the drama of being human into a simpler, more natural, essence. Breaking it down to not much more than a comatose heartbeat.

The poppy is a divinely seductive plant. Though the flower lasts for only a few days, the bulging seed pod holds an eternal true lover's magic. For eons, it has been used as an aphrodisiac and also to treat impotency and premature ejaculation. It's associations with the Goddess Aphrodite made the poppy a herb of choice for love charms and potions in connection with orgiastic rites and sex magic since the Middle Ages.

One would empty the seed capsule and write a question of the heart onto a piece of paper, put it into the seed pod, and place it underneath the pillow. The answer to one's question would be revealed in a dream.

≈

C an't make out the edges but it's moving. Blurred around the center like some Cartesian fractal. Jabbing at darkness to form a square. I reach towards it but touch nothing. It must be further away. Hanging in mid-air. Static. Pixelating. Throbbing. Woozing color that does not spill beyond its frame.

I'm blissfully groggy. It takes some time and effort to gain clarity. When it comes into focus, I realize I'm staring at a screen. The moving shapes take a little longer to pinpoint as they buzz around. They are horses, moving with speed around a racetrack. Sharp jockeys in neon shirts above the sprinting animals. Like they're eight bit animations above a four legged torpedo. Bouncing along towards a finish line then slowing to a gallop and canter.

Engaged in watching televised horse racing like it's Masterpiece Theater. And it is. With winners & losers and heroes & villains. Confirming that I'm in an opium den, lying on a mat, the one-eyed Chinaman approaches. He holds out a small pouch. It's tied with a golden string.

"Aah, you like the horse racing," he mutters.

"We too."

"In Hong Kong, everybody bets on horses. More than a million people betting every day."

"Big business. Big fun."

With slow motion precision, he untwirls the string on his purse. I notice that he is missing a finger.

He continues a one-way conversation. I smile and nod. He tells me about the famous horse races at the Royal Hong Kong Jockey Club. A storied history of the racetrack called Happy Valley, where, since 1884, they run the only race in town. All eyes on the sport. Everyone in Hong Kong is a horse racing aficionado. Over ten billion dollars a year. The Hong Kong Jockey Club takes in the same revenue as all horse race courses in the USA combined.

Horse racing was banned in mainland China, so Hong Kong was the popular place for the wealthy Chinese to gamble. Bribe an official on the mainland and get a weekend pass. All the gambling, prostitutes, and opium that you can fit into a few days before being stretchered back on the ferry ride back across the Pearl River Delta.

He offers the pouch to me balancing from an outstretched four-fingered hand.

"A gift."

I reach forward and take it with my own one-eyed smile. Leaning on one elbow, I open it, and out jumps a horse. A winged horse nonetheless.

And with some agility, I mount it, rising from the alcove balancing between wings with legs straddling horse flesh. Stuffing the pouch into my pocket, I brace myself for speed.

I hear a one-eyed voice trail off with some words about the winner's circle. Something about a tunnel that leads to my destination.

And we're off. Sauntering through the arches of the front gate.

Now we're full speed back down the narrow alleyways. Passing florists buffeted by high rise buildings. Through puddles I see my reflection ripple as hooves charge forward.

My excitement and my happiness are growing under the wings of a storm.

Reaching a busy intersection with merging traffic from all angles, we take flight over a rotunda. Swiftly gaining altitude, Pegasus rising. Lightning strikes. Confetti rain splashing through the skies.

As we approach, I recognize the building that I fled earlier that day and rise to meet her. Spiraling higher. Reaching for the top.

Unlit and sparse, it pulses with its own curse. A rear guard reflection. A vague recollection. Behind towering windows, the penthouse looks vacant. There is no sign of life. From above, the rooftop is an empty silicon chip. Pipes and wires intersecting then disappearing into blocks and cylinders.

Racing across the sky, through thick fog, an array of circular lights appears below. The lights of a stadium. The Hong Kong Jockey Club.

We descend mid-race following horses around the final turn, along the home stretch of the Happy Valley. We touch ground and materialize as the winners cross the finishing line.

A photographic finish. Flashes and applause everywhere.

Nonchalant, as if we finished third, I adjust goggles and helmet and cross in the direction of the stables.

There, I am drawn to a bust of a woman's head mounted on a wall of creeping ivy. Decades of growth ascends and descends from her stone head. She has hollow eyes. No eyeballs and leafy green serpents erupting from her brain like radioactive explosions.

Veering out of sight of the horse handlers around us, we trot towards the statue and read the quote on the plaque below.

> *"Deeper and deeper into Time's endless tunnel,*
> *does the winged soul, like a night-hawk,*
> *wend her wild way."*
> Herman Melville

Herman Melville wrote about the horses of the seas. He knew a horse was worth more than riches.

The wall of ivy is alive and it's not a wall at all. More like a draped serape. Within its shadowed creases, a rickety wooden stable door is hidden behind the overgrowth. Parting leaves, I notice a weathered copper handle, a rusted bolt, and key hole.

Instinctively, I reach into my pocket for the one-eyed Chinaman's pouch. In it, an eroded copper key that looks like it could open the Lost Ark of the Covenant. It unlocks the wooden doors. And as if forced by a gust from inside, they heave open.

We gallop through the entryway into the tunnel. Darkness all around. Only one way to go. Forward. We descend.

And now we're bolting into darkness. It all looks the same regardless whether eyes are open or closed. Pegasus in control. So smooth this ride, I might as well be on the back of a butterfly. Wings closed. I hold on. Surrender to the journey.

∾

If I die tonight, please do not deify me. I pray do not put me in a box in the ground. Etch me no headstone.

I want to be dumped in a landfill. More like a refuse mountain of things that no longer work. One that spreads its fringes wider day by day. And higher night by night as more dump trucks deliver more worthless waste. A living landfill for the dead.

Over time I'll be entombed in a manmade mountain range. Bring me all your plastic circles and squares blazoned with music. Records and CDs. Black like tar. Reflective like broken mirrors. This will be the final resting place for me and all the music of the twentieth century.

Adorning this mountain range, a glorious amalgamation of crevices and outcrops. Dangerous cliffs and epic valleys. Scenic vistas where nothing grows. The views will be panoramic.

I'll fuse with the billion units of records, cassettes, eight track tapes, and CDs that have been abandoned. This would make a perfect Shangri-La for me.

Amongst plastic scraps of music. Scratched and trashed and twisted and dented. Every single one of them. Eventually, the heat of the sun will forge us into one. One melted mass. Oozing. Dripping. Bubbling like the oil from which we originate. Returning to formlessness.

And in the shade of synthetic caverns, amongst the one hit wonders and 12" maxi singles, lay my body down on an oversized pillow stuffed with magnetic tape. Cushioned and comfortable, I will float amidst songs which were once embedded and ingrained in plastic and have now been set free to be carried down melted vinyl streams.

The history of music careening like treacle between my skeletal toes.

I'll arrive at a mausoleum molded and sculpted and wallpapered with album sleeves and liner notes. So I can rest with my brothers and sisters, all broken musicians that have passed. Wrap me in eight track tape and make a mummy of me. As this will be my final resting place.

God bless the mp3. From invisible clouds you reign. Destroyer of the physical unit. Hallowed be thy name. Harbinger of a new era. Sire of this monumental mountain range.

In the silence of this death, may our music live forever.

Taking no prisoners tonight in Miami. Gonna riot through this massive. Rip them a third eye. A silver bullet through the middle of the best of my record collection. Give them what they came here for. Tugging on heart strings with my greatest hits. A romantic sonic asphyxiation.

When ten thousand people yell for more and I play my own song, it's like thunder striking twice.

Sound is so powerful it can shatter glass. Move mountains. Leave a lifelong impression on a young heart.

Then it's signing posters and posing in the step and repeat with people I don't know. More pictures with fans against the barricade who don't know me. Fan girls looking like Polyester hell in vinyl pumps, Day-Glo lingerie, and neon hats. Ten times ten too many bracelets and bangles. Fashion made in China.

A word of advice: leave the vinyl to the DJs and the Tupperware in the fridge.

Grab my bag and I'm out the stage doors. Where's the town car? I'm ready for the after party. Need to re-script this insanity. Need some breathing room before we get down again. 'Cause the rave don't stop.

~

DJ S was a rising star five years ago. Famous in the local club scene. The scene changed. Career stalled. But he can still put together an after party. That's no easy feat.

I guess anyone can do it, if they've got enough friends, though there are essential ingredients without which it's not going to work. Work meaning be the cool place to hang out in the hours before and after sunrise.

Number One: Drugs. Anything illegal will do. A selection would be best. Some like it up and some like it down. Though I'd use some discretion if I was you. You don't really want to be wiping people off the floor. You wanna keep 'em on their toes. At least a little bit. Some like to mix and match in inventive ways. Give them a choice of designer pharmaceuticals. None of that over-the-counter crap. Maybe something couture that we have never tried before. Something with both letters and numbers that sounds like a license plate.

Number Two: Alcohol. Enough to last for days because we will run out. Beer and wine is fine but if you're clever then bourbon, rum, or tequila. Always top shelf. Leave the vodka at the club or hide it behind the celery until morning.

Number Three: A DJ rig. You won't be short of DJs. They'll be lining up. Could be fun testing ground for some newcomers or amateurs. Make sure you vet them first. Please no iPods or God-forbid Pandora. Online robots choosing your music could lead to some devastating ramifications. And a playlist is unacceptable. Could be disastrous. You need a human to steer. Banging it and breaking it down. And more of the latter please. We don't want to piss off the neighbors and get the cops involved. Cops don't like after parties unless they're in the mix. They'll be jealous of how much fun we're having and shut the music down.

Number Four: Freaky friends. If you don't have any then you need some new friends.

Oh there's one more aspect and this is crucial. A good mix of boys and girls. Got to keep it sexy and ambiguous. Regardless of your sexual preference, an even split will keep the eyes darting and bodies circulating. Keep them guessing on the improvised dance floor. Keep it fresh with some new blood. Dim the lights and you're good through dawn.

You wouldn't disappoint to add a few other accoutrements: bowls of grapes and strawberries, arrangements of flowers, unscented candles, nitrous oxide, a disco oil lamp, a slow flashing strobe.

A Jacuzzi is always welcome because it encourages nudity, and the fewer clothes, the better.

If you disagree with this list then you're probably a drug addict used to an inelegant mess and you're not invited to my house.

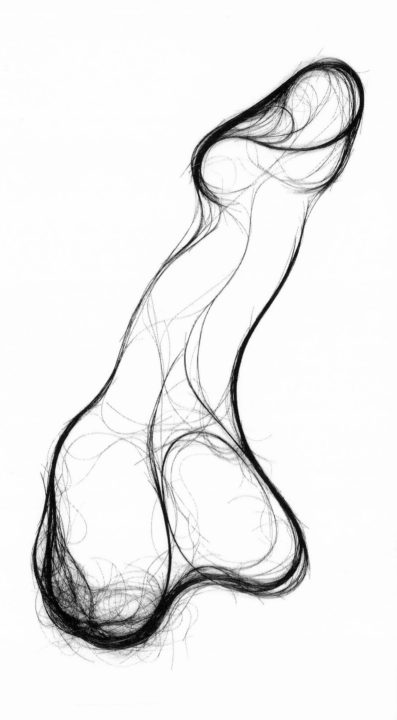

~

S's after party looks good at first glance. I grab a beer from the fridge. Spark a joint. Join a nearby conversation where versatile anecdotes are shared.

Deep beats from the living room. Bong and speckled mirror on the kitchen counter. A pewter plate with green buds next to it. Eager chatter and laughter all round. An opportunity to meet friends of friends outside the incessant noise of the club.

Every city has a fascinating collection of late night personalities. Long on individual traits. The lost. The found. All on the cusp of greatness. Some about to fall.

Edgy and sharp are the characteristics of double edged swords.

After a few drinks, I notice the party is short on girls. I've been talking about music for long enough to realize that I'm talking about music. Besides the innocuous DJ's girlfriend, only one girl catches my eye.

All four feet of her have been circulating like a penguin. Coalescing. Mingling. Rubbing skin.

Gorgeously mis-proportioned in all the right places, she talks in squeals. Pitched up like a cartoon character. Exaggerated like a spokesperson for herself. Too much eye shadow and concealer. Too many holes in her ears. She prefers to talk than listen.

Thankfully she's not too vacant and has a sense of humor. She knows a thing or two. She designed herself with borrowed traits. Mimicking young Hollywood starlets as if a camera was following her moves.

Some girls learn all their stuff from TV. Clearly she has had some first-hand experience. She didn't arrive at being this coquettish by watching reality shows and sitcoms or spying on her elder sister. She has confidence born of living to the limit.

I'm not the only one who has noticed her. There are several guests who have won her attention.

As if by some feminine legerdemain, she corrals a few of us up some stairs into an attic area. She's holding court. All eyes on her and she loves it. There are no chairs or any other furniture. Like electrons, we form a circle around her. Watching her vacillate between coy and pomp. There is an electric charge in the air. Like a charged atom, the energy grows. Circles are powerful. They hold space. They attract and repel.

She pulls a handkerchief from mid-air and cheerfully blindfolds herself. She has this look like Bambi in heat. All smutty and beckoning. And there, another handkerchief and someone is binding her hands behind her back in a way that's uncomfortable but not cruel. Two more heads pop up the stairs and we're now seven surrounding her. She's faking trying to wiggle free.

She starts veering side to side like a bumper car slowly bouncing within the circle. Like we're playing Ouija board with her and it starts getting rougher in a playful kind of way. There's no escaping even if she wants to, which she doesn't. She delights in the fracas as her shirt is tugged and pulled, eventually ripping. A button cascades onto the floor and rolls towards me. Circles several times then stops. I pick it up.

Now she's in the middle. Stationary. Solitary. Waiting for the next move. And our host whips out his cock and steps forth like he's entering a rodeo. His hand grips below her chin and he thrusts it into her mouth which is waist high.

It's in and out in a second. She's probing for more. Mouth open. He dips in again this time deeper. She gurgles and grunts and when he's out again she laughs.

And one by one, each take a turn with her. She's lapping it up like a thirsty mule. Saliva dripping. Thick and elastic. None of the guys can believe what's going on. Teenage smirks all over faces. It's a circular jerk off with her in the middle, and one by one, without any doubt or shame, they go at her. She doesn't know which direction it will come from next.

She's naked from the waist up. Large pear shaped breasts protrude unevenly through her misaligned bra. One nipple squeezed upwards by the strap. Untampered tight pants cannot hide the moisture of her own excitement. The pants stay on as each one comes on her. All over her chin. Her cheeks. Her hair. Her cleavage. Glazing her face in a plastic sheen. A protective coat of come.

Why can't I take my eyes off her? And when I can't take staring anymore, I rush towards the stairs. To further etch the scene in my memory, I glance one more time over my shoulder at her lacquered image.

What do I see? I see a raggedy girl with matted hair and a glossy confident smirk, barefoot on toes, willing and ready to take more.

Minutes later, I'm in the town car, heading back to the hotel.

"They definitely needed more girls at that party," says the driver.

Fingering the button from her shirt between thumb and forefinger, I vocally agree.

There's a thought. A regret. A needle through the buttonholes riveting my finger. As the button dances between thumb and forefinger, the needle digs deeper.

I wish I had taken her with me. Leaving her there was a betrayal.

She displayed such boldness. An audacity that is hard to come by. I wonder how she uses that prowess in her life. At work or at school. To get what she wants. To find pleasure. To pleasure others.

The button is binding itself to my finger. There is the faint throbbing of a distant heartbeat as the needle sews into my skin.

Perhaps she doesn't use that boldness at all. Perhaps she doesn't own her power. It may be wasted on torrential strangers in attics at after parties.

However, for a brief moment, when the group thought she was the prey, she was fully in control. She had subverted the dominant. Reversed control. She had all the power.

I'd like to have her back in my hotel room. Watch her closely as she comes down from her performance high.

Untwist. Undress. Unglue.

I would help clean her hair with bubbles, watch her shiver on the bathroom mat between bath and towel, then possess her with an intimacy that would make her come before she finds herself again.

~

I've got the soul of a woman.
The spirit of a man.
The heart of your sister.
Beating close to mine.

C an't decide what to eat so I ask for both. And I wash it
down with a beer.

Always hearing wallpaper music proposing to me from
behind walls. Sometimes the verse is catchier than the chorus.
I prefer that it only repeats once.

"Wanna split an E?"

"OK."

She twists a capsule and gives it to me. I pop it in my
mouth and swallow.

"Where's my half?" she says.

"Didn't you give me half?"

"No, dumbass, you were supposed to bite it in half!"

"Shit. Sorry."

All right, let's go. Game starts in about thirty minutes. May take a little longer since I just ate. It's better on an empty stomach.

Revealing conversations that I'll never remember are started. Tangents are welcome. Segue into ten new conversations. You can really get to know people this way. They tend to open up. If they are awkward it may mean that they are attracted to you.

Bedroom dances with strangers. Staggers forward, lurches back. Surprised nothing gets knocked off.

A DJ plays his maxi-minimal sounds.

Jackets and shoes collect in the corners. Drinking all the beers and smoking all the smokes. Then another layer.

There's blackjack in the kitchen. Six around the table. Winner gets to shuffle. Eggs are cooked quicker than a round at this table.

Accents are thick. Words garbled. Foam collects and hardens around the dealer's upper lip.

Conversations start like this. "I got fired from my new job at a gay porn production company for getting caught with coke at the door of The End Up."

"Want a bump?"

Gentle shoulder rub.

Take off another layer.

Yes please. Tap water is OK.

"Great set tonight," whispers in my ear.

"The police stopped by to check the cabaret license of the venue. Had to lower the decibels and keep them dancing."

"I was in the red."

Laughter.

In excess.

You're one of my kind ... hallucinate ... fabricate ...

Surprised I didn't lose anything. Jackets and headphones often slip away unnoticed.

She tells me she has ghosts in her house. Asks if I want to see. Then scrolls through pics on her phone and stops at one of her in a bra. Then another with no bra. She points to the ghost in the background.

I need you tonight … 'cause I'm not sleeping.

Another layer.

Shorter sentences.

"You look great."

One word answers.

Smiles all around.

Hair like silk.

Lips like kisses.

Bubbling up.

Like molecules.

Getting warmer in here.

Somebody opened up the oven. Cranked the heat. I'm rising. Everyone is too.

And there's this spontaneous moment triggered by the music where the pants come off. Everyone's dropping clothes. Stripping down to underwear.

The pants-off dance-off has started.

Some are prepared. With g-strings and the tiniest briefs. Others caught unaware in baggy boxers. But everyone is down to the minimum as we shuffle dance to the minimal ping pong beat.

She's swaying in her daddy's tighty-whitey briefs. He's spun out in his lover's fishnet tights. Not a rip anywhere near enough to divulge the bulge.

There's passion on the improvised dance floor. Serious sexual signals bouncing off the ceiling. High as kites. Gliding.

Ecstatic sweat dripping from necks to glistening navels onto the bamboo floor.

Feet slip and slide. It's wide open.

His flesh feels warm and smooth to her. Her swelling breasts are looking for hands. Eyes dilated and head in the clouds, the room is flickering like a feast in a Fellini film.

In the back of the DJ's mind she's wondering, Jesus Christ, how to calm things down because it's provocative chaos. Through the shutters, it's soon light outside and the kids may be coming home from their sleepover.

And then it booms and snaps. Loud as fuck. Three entwined bodies collide with the tempered glass record shelf and it all comes tumbling down. Little chunks of broken glass and sprawling flesh and hundreds of records on the floor.

A heap of a mess that looks like a million diamonds. The fantasy of night has shattered into the reality of day.

～

A rriving at the venue after the smooth ride from Hong Kong harbor tunneling through mountains to the countryside, it's a ranch or something. A line of distinguished vehicles waiting to enter. There's a row of Rolls Royces. Ghosts, Clouds, Phantoms, and Shadows.

We are waved through security at the front gate. Around a bend we slow down. A woman with a stickered clipboard comes over.

"You the DJ?"

"Yeah."

"Do you have any preconceived notions of tonight's event?"

"No."

"Has anyone told you anything now or at any time leading up to your arrival here, any information, about this event?"

"Em … no."

"Welcome. This is a private event. Please refrain from taking any photos or recordings."

~

So I've made it to the gig. The reason I'm in Hong Kong in the first place. Hired to play music tonight at a high society wedding. What a whirlwind it's been. Still trying to get some dose of reality. Some perspective. Unlikely. Everything is already sideways and revolving.

Hong Kong is an archipelago. Made up of almost two hundred islands. Ink spots on a map. We took the tunnel from the Happy Valley on Hong Kong Island through Sham Shui Po to Lantau Island. Rode through mountain passes and tunnels to reach our final destination.

My chaperone has given me a little history of Hong Kong and some background on where we're heading. An inside scoop into the scale of the wedding and what it means to the families involved.

Holding tightly to her torso, I kept dozing off while she talked.

Her words splinter and jerk as I process the whizzing foreign landscape. Eyes half aware. Wind whistling through the holes in my head.

Here's what I recall.

Hong Kong became a British Colony after the First Opium War in the early 1800s. A port of illegal trade. Recently Britain returned it to China in 1997. Through all this time a few powerful families controlled the trade ways. Some British. Others Chinese. The British called the Chinese gangs the Triads. They stem from age old underground family led organizations with colorful names like The Heaven and Earth Society and The White Lotus Society.

To this day, the Triads engage in all kinds of criminal activity from extortion and money laundering to trafficking and prostitution. They are involved in smuggling and counterfeiting cheap Chinese goods like music, video, and software and exporting them around the world.

Those $19 fake Oakley sunglasses that I bought from an ad on Facebook, which were shipped directly from China, were probably made in Triad controlled factories.

The Triads are like Mafia clans and they also control gambling. Macau, an island west of Hong Kong, is the gambling center of the East. In the center of Hong Kong, the Royal Hong Kong Jockey Club is the urban hub for local gambling. A convenient epicenter for mega-money laundering. It's run as a non-profit organization with billions passing through each year. The Royal Hong Kong Jockey Club is the largest private charitable donor and the largest taxpayer in all of Hong Kong. Ka-ching! They know how to keep everyone happy in the Happy Valley.

If I remember correctly what my chaperone told me, the bride-to-be is a descendant of one of the primary benefactors of the Opium Wars. Fourth generation wealth. Rich, young, and naive, she represents a new wave. Twenty-first century carefree international vibes and don't-give-a-fuck attitude. It's a struggle to leave a legacy behind. The well-heeled groom is older and positioned to head his family business. He will take control of massive fortunes if he plays his cards right. Their marriage, a union of two powerful dynasties, would be his coup de grace.

Some would like to believe in the merit of this marriage. Some believe it to be an orchestrated business arrangement. There are those who would prefer it not to happen. Some have a lot to lose. Everyone has an opinion. There are family members on both sides who have more than the couple's well being in mind. And there are external forces too. Anyone who is anyone in Hong Kong society will be arriving in Rolls Royces, raising flutes of Dom Perignon to congratulate the newly married couple, while, at the same time, casting aspersions around the dinner table.

Gavin Hardkiss

∿

I'm used to landing in a circus atmosphere. Cartwheels and handstands. Punctuated laughter and canned shenanigans. Bowler hats can't hide those red noses from further alcoholic abuse. Sparkling sequins and tuxedo bow ties. Appearing elegant to only those who are dressed the same.

Tamed wild animals are here for the food and drink. Wild social climbers are here for the tricks. High drama unfolding.

I'm a joker on the high wire. A trapeze artist amongst clowns with no net to save me when I fall. In fact, I'm in free fall now. Even though I can't see the net from these dizzy heights, I have convinced myself that it's there. When I look down on all these clowns, I'm not afraid. And if I fall, I fall on top of them and we all fall down.

I'm no lion tamer but I can tie a balloon in the shape of a lion, squeeze it through an RCA audio cable into an amplifier connected to loudspeakers which, at the speed of sound, transforms something tame and childlike into a roar in their ears.

Invisible high heels. I'll have them dancing on their toes in no time.

The situation is not foreign. I'm used to stretching my luck in unknown territory. Whenever I approach the end of my tightrope, it mysteriously gets longer like a vine growing before me. Just like Jack and his magic beans, I'll save the day even if I have to wrestle with a giant tycoon or two.

The politics of this situation goes in one ear and out the other.

I'm a minstrel disguised as a DJ who is really the jester in the court of the aristocracy. I'm here to have fun and hell I hope they are too.

∾

The woman with the clipboard and the earpiece approaches. Holds out a hand. Introduces herself. She explains the wedding time line. I get the picture. I'll be DJing in the courtyard after dinner.

The courtyard has been meticulously staged. There's up lighting and spot lighting and draped clusters of ornamental strings of LED lights, rows of hanging lanterns which cascade from six elevated angles to join an ornate crystal chandelier in the middle. Like a luminous octopus that can change color and sway in the current. A team of lighting professionals put this together. Many late night meetings in design studios with draft boards were spent finalizing this set-up and spending the money. Lighting tricks to elevate the mood for various intervals in tonight's program.

Lace and silk hanging from banisters. Neon signs with Chinese characters articulate the stone walls within the courtyard. Attempting to look like Shanghai in the '20s, it all looks a bit '80s.

After dinner the tables will be cleared and heating lamps will be repositioned to the periphery, providing an intimate space for barefoot dancing on a giant oriental rug. The rug looks like it has fondled the manicured toenails of royalty in centuries past. Rubbed raw in sideways patterns.

A floor level DJ rig is hidden behind an altar decorated with fantastic flowers. Arrangements with blooms, bamboo, bark, and Bryophyta.

Each element simply positioned, its stalk and leaves adding meaning in a conversation with twigs and petals to form a fantastical forest. Water flows over a melted plastic Yamaha concert keyboard and cascades into drums shaped like a pan flute. Plastic characters interplay amongst the fluorescent moss with taxidermied hummingbirds, dragonflies, and bees hovering.

Squadrons and platoons in position to defend me.

~

There is an ancient Eastern art form called Hanakotoba which is the language of flowers. In this practice plants are given codes and passwords. The flowers convey emotion and communicate directly to each other. They are arranged in a way to convey specific meaning. Physiological effects predicate action in the presence of a variety of features including the presence of color, thorns, medicinal properties, and the smell of the flowers. The arrangement can be used to send secret messages. Illicit subconscious persuasion to prompt a response.

Some flowering plants have a sexual orientation that switches from generation to generation. Some orchids are hermaphrodites and they have evolved to be able to fertilize themselves.

Catch them at the right time and you might bear witness to the multiple love making positions of the flowers. Catch the right angle and you might see a rainbow in that waterfall.

Notice this floral composition in various acts of sexual intercourse with its parts and you might feel aroused.

There are three classes of people. Those who see it. Those who see it when they are shown it. Those who do not see it at all.

I could stare at this installation for hours. I want to climb into it. And I will be behind it in a few hours but until then I need to find some nourishment and something to pick me up otherwise I'll crossfade.

If I manage to keep my eyes open for the next few hours, I can stay awake until my flight leaves tomorrow. I've had plenty of practice at this.

~

A Zoologist who studies the sound of animals is called a Zoomusicologist. That's a long word, which they should have shortened to Zoomologist because that looks and sounds better.

A Zoomologist understands the miscellaneous sounds that make up an animal's vocabulary. They play recordings over a loudspeaker and witness changes in animal behavior. They learn to prompt behavior by playing a sequence of sounds. David Attenborough told me that there is a vocalization that you can do in a forest in the middle of nowhere which will make Petrel birds fall from the trees to the ground. The sound intoxicates the birds and I might use that trick tonight.

Playback a recording of a lioness in heat and it will get the male's attention even when he's asleep. Get him prowling around looking for pleasure. Arousal can be generated by sound.

You just got to know which sounds to play. And in which order.

It turns out that music is a widespread phenomenon in several living species apart from man. This calls into question the definition of music. Some human languages don't even have a word for music. This is true for a variety of indigenous tribes including some in North American and West African.

We understand music to be an arrangement of sounds and silences. A sequence of sounds that is pleasing. If it was unpleasant we would call it noise but that's a matter of interpretation.

Does music exist in the world without the human listener? Is it the listener's experience that defines the music?

We call sounds made by nature, like the sound of a waterfall or wind through reeds, musical. There is no need for melody or a pattern to be musical. Ever hear a hummingbird fly past your ear? Or the sound of stones in a river which may be of comfort enough to lull you into a deeper meditation.

Hear the groan and stretch of a tree before it falls and will you be scuttling for cover or listening a little closer?

Language can be musical with its own nuanced intonations. Words peppered with subtle articulation differ from region to region. Listening to a foreign language in a foreign land may be a blissful symphony to one person and a disquieting threat to another.

Music does not need a translator.

Is music purely the experience of the pleasure derived from sound? Is it the cognitive and emotive response that we experience through sound? What is music to animals? What is music to plants?

I don't know.

~

Watching a wedding ceremony ought to be a comforting experience. Though the idea of two souls colliding and staying fixed together for life is absurd. The fact that people sign up for it gives me hope in the greater good of humankind.

But it's the absurdity that I'm after. I enjoy the brittleness of the moment. Like something could crack. Yolk running down the aisle and ruining those silly bridesmaids' dresses.

Moms' and dads' aged expressions expose a hint of sadness behind the oblique pride – "Kids all grown up now, so what does that make us?" Older and sliding further down.

Moments like this belie a truth that the grandeur of the event cannot hide. And the more ostentatious the wedding, the more there is to cover up. And the more there is to prove. Making up for lost time. Making up for lovelessness.

I won't ask whose idea it was to have a Masonic sacrificial ceremony. Probably the father, who may be up there in the twenty somethingth Masonic degree and he probably knows a few things that we don't. I can only wonder. But someone just lugged a pig over their shoulder into the heart of this wedding. This is going to be different.

～

A nd here is what I witness, off to the side from proximity, with eyes wide open.

The groom enters in a flowing white dress full of folds and curls and takes his seat. The veiled bride comes in afterward and takes her seat to the left of the groom. They are separated by a piece of cloth held between them as a curtain, so that they may not see each other.

A priest follows dressed in an embroidered golden robe with an impressive jeweled head dress that looks like its from the Ming Dynasty. He has three servants to assist him. One holds a bowl with burning incense. One holds an empty bowl. One holds a sword pointing up in outstretched hands.

The bride's and groom's hands are joined and the curtain is held over the hands. The priest takes a long golden rope and begins to encircle the couple, literally, tying them together seven times.

The priest is muttering and singing in some strange dialect that has no resemblance to anything I have heard before.

Tension mounts.

The priest now ties their joined hands. He fastens them with a raw twist of thin golden string, which he winds seven times.

He belts out a chanting prayer that the Gods will have no choice but to pay close attention to, and then follows it with words that I understand.

"May the Creator, the Omniscient Lord, grant you a progeny of sons and grandsons, plenty of means of provision, heart-ravishing friendship, bodily strength, long life, and an existence of 150 years."

Then the pig is carried in front of the groom. The servant delivers the sword to the groom's right hand and the groom slashes the animal's neck in one twist of the wrist. Just like that. As if he's had many occasion to practice. The blood of the animal gushes into the bowl held by a servant below.

I feel the blood pressure rise in my finger as the priest dips his forefinger into the bowl. Continuing a rising blood-curdling chant, the priest moves in to draw a line with the blood on the forehead of the groom. Reaching through the parted veil, he draws a circle on the forehead of the bride.

Then he asks the bride, "Have you and your family with righteous mind, and truthful thoughts, words, and actions, and for the increase of righteousness, agreed to give, forever, yourself in marriage to this man?"

She whispers: "I have agreed."

Then the priest asks the groom, "Have you preferred to enter into this contract of marriage up to the end of your life with righteous mind?"

He replies: "I have preferred."

The priest takes a bushel of fern leaves, dips it in the bloody bowl and begins to spray it. Moving back and forth in the four cardinal directions, blood sprays on the ground and on nearby guests. It's unbelievable. Everyone cheers. They revel in the blood ritual.

Like ink, the dots of blood absorb fast and dry.

What is the symbolism of a blood ritual? The blood and the smoky incense evoke a benediction for the ages. An ancient, long forgotten ritual which will impress the millionaires and appease the Gods. An ultimate experience. An indelible memory.

Blood marks the birth/death equation. XY as coordinates that meet at one point in the presence of the Holy.

The priest announces, "We have witnesses," and then concludes, "By the powers vested in me I now proclaim you husband and wife."

The X and Y axis have momentarily intersected. The XX and XY chromosomes will merge sometime later.

But I don't stick around for this theater to end with a profane kiss because I don't want any more blood spilled on me.

~

E xhausted sitting on the runway. Gotta get comfortable because I'm gonna be here awhile. It's like sardines and I need to get some rest. Elbow to elbow. Elbow chess. Bishop to queen. She counter moves. Check.

Two inches of real estate. Wrists rub against the bangled forearm of the girl next to me. Queen to bishop. Checkmate.

"Sorry," she mutters.

"Sorry," I repeat without looking.

Head back, I breathe the stale air littered with too many fragrances. Cheap or expensive, they all stink. There's one fragrance that counterbalances the cacophony. Brings some order. Her odor is that of oats. As if she had been rolling around in a field earlier today.

And with head back, I sink a little bit. And, like a lullaby, it lulls me into a comfort zone.

Lucky she isn't fat. Lucky she smells good.

Gonna be here for a while so I might as well relax. My legs soften. Thigh brushing thigh. And it's about as close as one could get to a perfect stranger. Elbow to elbow. Wrist to wrist. Thigh to thigh. Breathing each other.

And this is where I drift off into a shallow sleep. Pleasant thoughts of fetish ripple through my consciousness. Ice on flesh. Erect nipples. Bed knobs of a four post bed penetrate chambermaids as I lie on the sheets unfurled like a cat.

And as I drift in and out of wakefulness, it's the tingling ends of waist length hair uncurling next to me that tickle my inner elbow and whisk me back. Like a feather duster wiping webs from untended corners.

Eyes open. We make eye contact for the first time. Smile and chat about small insignificant things as if we had planned travel together and had booked these seats in advance.

Hard to tell how old a woman is by looking at her. Seventeen to thirty-five is blurred and obscured or luminous and bright depending on how well she takes care of herself. Self-esteem can make her seem either younger or older depending on her whim. Some teenagers look like women before their time. Everyone is different. I don't purport to know or care about age.

Obviously choice of dress and jewelry goes a long way but never tells the entire story. That's the beauty of fashion. More so what it conceals than what it reveals.

Ripped jeans are not reserved for teenage fashion. A good pair of ripped jeans is expensive. Unless you make them yourself. But it's unlikely that you'll get it right the first time. Equally expensive to experiment with the process

Some women will pay $400 for rips in all the right places. Someone somewhere went to fashion school to learn how to make ripped jeans. It's a modern art form. Well-sized rips in the right direction.

Light abbreviated chatter turns to talk about casinos. Games of chance. Winners and losers. Thankfully no long winded personal stories that reveal too much.

Vagueries. Innuendos. Not enough to seem forward or suggestive. But one can read it that way. Enough to make a red eye far from dull.

As the cabin lights slip off and the other passengers slide into their own dreams, we continue in hushed tones with muted enthusiasm.

Sometime soon I have to crash. And it's blankets unfolded. Masks on. Reading lights off.

And it's at this point that we hit a patch of turbulence. Enough to make your stomach creep. And the plane dips. Almost dives.

She grabs my thigh. Fingers like tendrils long and reaching. I hoist the armrest between us and reciprocate. Fingers coiling forward beneath the blanket onto her thigh, finding stone-washed cotton threads that reveal thin patches of skin.

She is compliant.

The plane lurches.

As my fingers explore the fabric, picking it apart like a guitar, balance is restored. Softly strumming the frets between the strings, I feel her do something remarkable.

Like a kneading lynx, she cleverly claws her way through my jeans. I didn't know they were frayed over there. Surgically, she sears through the material gashing my skin. But only slightly. Nearly enough to make me wince.

Singlehandedly we explore each other's most sensitive inner thigh. As if each of our hands, my left and her right, belong to the same sentient creature that is neither of us.

On the surface, we are like the other three hundred and fifty-two passengers. Resting in a speeding tin can ten thousand meters above the earth. Beneath the blankets, there's a wild carnivorous creature on the hunt. Creeping, soundlessly deeper into the thickest most dangerous humid jungle.

Fingers rip through material. Pulling at edges. Leveraging strings. Kneading and twisting. Groping in the dark in a race to see who can be the slowest and most unnoticeable.

There is little reprieve from the tension. Though we both keep our outer cool. Only we can feel the tension mount. It's all so calculated but not. One follows the other's move. An unexpected pitch or tug or clasp sends splinters up and down both spines. Olympic restraint.

Millimeters seem like miles.

And we scissor through reaching undergarments at precisely the same time. I ferret through a thick tuft of bush that panties cannot hide. Curling and unfurling between finger tips. Digging in where hair meets satin meets flesh to cross the last line of defense. Fingers descend and pry open.

Ensnaring, coiling, re-coiling, suffocating, releasing, prying, mangling.

The smell of oats is sweeter now and the faintest sound of a whimper can be heard not far away.

~

Nosing around the grounds after the ceremony. I find a private area that looks subversive. Subterranean. Like old servant's quarters. A Mandarin styled basement with revisionist colonial furnishings. Dark with ornate lamps casting deep shadows on the red velvety wallpaper. Dip down stairs and enter the room, bending to avoid banging my head on the low ceiling in the entryway.

There's a poker hand of characters in a loaded deck that has not been shuffled. I pin them as family members. They flock around a low wooden table, below the revolutions of a single blade ceiling fan, in scattered conversation. Ashtrays, iced tumblers, and narco fanfare litter the surface.

They are a tantalizing collection of the best post-colonial blood that Hong Kong has to offer. Light skinned heirs and heiresses who huddle in deference to each other.

He's got New York teeth. He wears his asshole on his sleeve. Sometimes he cries to his dead mother when he's coming down from drugs. In his fevered sleep there's a fire hydrant which he can never loosen. Everything's ablaze, burning to the ground. In his hand a smoldering match. He never supports the underdog. Kicks them when they're down or when no one is looking. If he was a disease he'd be Lyme disease. Difficult to pin down even when you know the symptoms. He starts a lot of sentences "I hate it when …." Then laughs.

She's a cruel joke on herself. There's no punch line. She has Vina del Sol for breakfast. Shots of Botox for lunch. She breaks her virginity regularly. It crashes and splinters when it hits the floor. If she was a disease she'd be Gonorrhea. Symptoms appear a month later, hiding the perpetrator in a Galliano leather cloak in the shadows of the distant past. She's like a bat that pretends to like sweet fruit, when all she wants is your blood. Or more wine.

He's a drunk. Drunk and always sweating. A pockmarked face that recalls the surface of the moon. Rocky. Granular. Protruding. Unexplored craters that hide signs of life. Signs of life that hide untapped reservoirs of oil. Hold a flame too close to his face and it will explode. This happened once before and left permanent dark stained soot beneath his eyes. He has since given up smoking, but his clothes hold on to that scent like a perfume gift from a lost lover.

She's a very successful trader. Traded punches and lovers to get to the top. A black diamond. Bewilderingly beautiful. Impossible to crack. She'll etch her mark on the toughest surface. Her elegant billowing Chanel ball gown hides a leather girdle with a strap on dildo. It's all lady-like-polite-smiles until you let down your guard and then she'll fuck you up the ass. You didn't know you'd like it so much, so you grant her your favor and break away from your family to see her anytime she's in town.

They all know each other all too well. Cut from the same cloth. Sons and daughters of corrupt colonial fortunes. The apple doesn't fall far from the tree.

I know this type. Never really had to work a day in their lives. But high society requires that they perform in some way. Fortune favored them to be born to their parents. They have a duty to navigate the mess of wealth in a way to legitimize their progeny. Placed well in society, doors always open in the right direction, so long as they play by the rules. The rules are murky. But the bottom line is that no one wants to get cut off from inheritance and trust funds so the wanderlust and the rebellious types subvert their own curiosity into darker agendas.

I'm like the joker in their straight flush. They welcome me in with a bat of an eyelash and a cock of the chin. I'm more interested in the wall behind them which is aglow with phonographs neatly stacked on spines. There are thousands of records wall to wall and floor to ceiling.

I could get comfortable in here with these scumbag bankers, tramps, and addicts and all these delectable records.

Gavin Hardkiss

~

The conversation begins like this.

"Who are you?"

"I'm the DJ."

"Fuck off."

Then from the rear of the room.

"Don't be a pig to every stranger," a sandy woman's voice says to him.

Then to me she says, "Don't listen to a word he says. He's an asshole. This family is full of them."

Initially, I hadn't noticed her in the shadowy under light off to the side. I slide off behind the others towards her more welcoming direction.

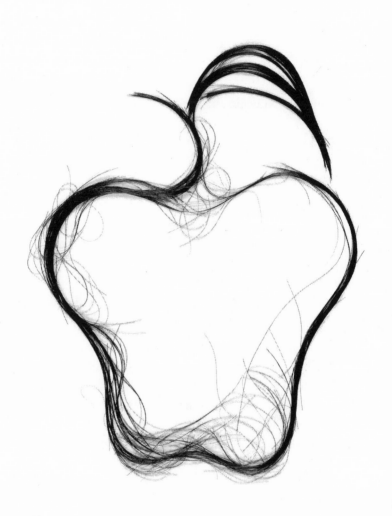

~

E verybody knows that the apple doesn't fall far from the tree. This, however, is a metaphor that doesn't hold true for all trees. For example, the Tree of Knowledge. Intelligence is not dispersed equivocally to successive generations. There are unpredictable gaps.

However, if the tree was a money tree, then crisp bundles of banknotes have been falling neatly into clinical piles for select families in Hong Kong since The Opium War of 1842.

"Is this your first time in Hong Kong?" asks Oilface with elocution dribbling through the pressure of a pumpjack.

"Yeah."

"And you've slid into the inner sanctum. All credit to you," says Lyme.

"It's an occupational hazard and an honor." I laugh. "Sliding into private places."

"Tell me about this place." I ask, settling in a bit, "Tell me about Hong Kong. I want to know about opium and Hong Kong."

"Ha. Getting right to the point I see. We have to start in the eighteenth century then," says Lyme.

"It's a long story which begins with Britain's thirst for tea. You see, the Queen and her subjects were buying boatloads of tea from China and the Chinese didn't want any British crap in return. A disturbing trade imbalance grew as Britain drained its silver deposits to keep up with the royal demand for tea."

"Trading ships en route from Europe to China would stop in India and pick up cargoes of opium harvested in the Golden Triangle. And so began the scourge as the Chinese developed an unhealthy appetite for the opium high."

Lyme grabs a tumbler of gin and tonic and slurps a mouthful. A small cube of ice rattles against his teeth before he crushes it and continues.

"The British Freemason lodges acted as safe houses for the opium traders. The drugs were smuggled in through these lodges using a network of organized criminal families like the Triads, the Hong Society, and the Assassins. Thus the British sponsored a mass addiction to opium until Chinese society and vitality was practically torn apart. The strategy used by the British in China has become a blueprint for invasion-by-drug-addiction since."

His accent is aristocratic and drips with self importance. His posture is animalistic like he could pounce and bite. His knowledge is encyclopedic and he likes you to know it.

Outside a wind whips through the garden. Drooping on high wires, lanterns creek and rattle. Umbrellas twist and turn. I can hear them flapping as if preparing for flight.

Meanwhile, in the foreground the history lesson continues.

"When the Chinese rulers acted to stop the opium supply, the British used their military and naval might to defeat them. In 1839, our great great grandfather William Jardine, a Canton-based opium trafficker, steered Britain into the first Opium War after Chinese officials confiscated his stash."

"And the 'peace' treaty after the conflict then gave the British a guaranteed right to increase the flow of opium; to be paid compensation for the opium the Chinese rulers had confiscated; and to have sovereignty over strategic ports and offshore islands and this is how Hong Kong came under British rule."

Between tugs on her Benson & Hedges, Strapon adds, "Hong Kong was used as the center for Far East drug trafficking and that is still its role today. Most of the gold and money transactions on the Hong Kong financial markets are the payoffs and money laundering of the global drug trade. Columbian, Mexican, and Russian cartels do their banking here."

Gonorrhea uncrosses her legs and gets into the conversation with a slurring, "In the aftermath of the Opium War, some debonair opium trading Scotsmen – who happened to be Freemasons too – set up the Hong Kong Shanghai Bank to safeguard our financial profits."

"Today, Jardine Matheson, our family's legacy, is Hong Kong's largest trading house and owns a major chunk of Hong Kong real estate."

"Like every second building."

"And the Hong Kong Shanghai Bank is now called HSBC and is the second-largest bank in the world. It runs and rigs the gold market. It is a safe haven for illicit hidden transactions by countries like Iran looking to skirt sanctions. It is still the world's number one drug money laundry."

"Not to mention that HSBC prints the Hong Kong Dollar," corroborates Strapon.

"Dazzling! The bank that was created to safehouse the profits of the opium trade still gets to print the local currency almost 150 years later," laughs Oilface.

Stubbing out one cigarette and lighting another, Strapon says, "One of the city's oldest clichés is that Hong Kong is run by Jardine Matheson, the Hong Kong Bank, the Jockey Club, and the governor – in that order."

"The governor got the boot when the Brits lost their lease in 1997. And the Hong Kong Bank is now HSBC. And the wealth still swirls in and out of the pockets of the descendants of a bygone colonial era. The Chinese have their hands in it now but we have strategic partnerships that keep everyone happy. There more than enough money to go round."

"What do you do with all this money?" I ask.

"Financial fetish. Whatever we want we can have," she continues without a drop of irony.

"The game is to keep the game going," quips Lyme Disease.

"Distraction and sleight of hand. Everyone is blinded by the headlights of headlines and breaking news. As long as the minions are entertained with their horse racing and celebrity-attention-span then we can continue with our boring lives unnoticed."

And then from nowhere, "Fucking where did that outsider come from. Never featured before."

~

For a second I think he's talking about me and my curiosity.

"My brother's upset since he lost his stupid bet this afternoon," says the sandy voice. "He missed the Triple Trio. Lost half a mil. A virtual unknown came in third and crashed his party."

She's obscured in an armchair with its back to me. Behind her, floor to ceiling windows open up to the lawns of a garden. Beyond, a grove of flowering trees ripples into the hills.

"Everybody thinks they're a winner. Lest we forget, horse racing is a game of chance."

"No different than the stock market," adds Oil Face.

"My brother used to be a stock market speculator. Then it was commodities. Then futures. Now he has the same team of actuaries and computer scientists working on computer models predicting race results. Mitigating risk. Probability crunching. Technology is propelling horse gambling into new territories. It sometimes works. Not today though."

"Racing has become more like the stock market. You can follow a horse and chart its progress like you would follow Apple or IBM."

I grab a pile of finger sandwiches from the sideboard.

"Do you gamble?" she inquires.

"Only with my life."

She laughs with a honk.

"How's that working for you? Are you successful?"

I wax. "This world does not need more 'successful people.' We need more peacemakers, healers, and lovers. We need people to live well in their rightful places. My idea of what success is has little to do with success as our culture has defined it."

"That's profound," she utters.

"I stole it from the Dalai Lama." I chuckle.

"Here in Hong Kong everybody gambles. It's an accepted part of society. I think it's a sickness," she continues.

"It doesn't hurt anyone!" her brother yells.

"People get their kicks in different ways, you know," I offer in between mouthfuls.

"How do you get your kicks?" she inquires matter-of-factly.

"Mmm, I have a vinyl fetish. I collect records. There are thousands of them in storage somewhere."

I walk up to the handcrafted cherry wood mantelpiece with its tsunami of records on display. Turntables built into a lower shelf. A discerning collection with a connoisseur DJ rig.

Fingering through the plastic sleeves I catch a glimpse of classics and obscure titles. From different eras. Mutations from different fragments of the world. A veritable cross section of someone's interpretation of history. From Eastern to Western. African to South American. Indefinable seminal moments of New Wave, Krautrock, J-pop, Samba Jazz, '80s Hip Hop, Go Go Funk, Afro Disco, Detroit Techno, and many regional micro genres invented to describe the gaps between.

"You don't see this much anymore," I say.

"It's as if music has been locked away. Seeing records out in the open like this is like public nudity. It's exciting."

"What do you mean 'locked away'?" a voice asks.

"Well, there was a time, not long ago, when everyone had a private record or CD collection. You could learn a lot about a stranger rifling through a collection. Tastes. Influences. Political leaning. People would keep them stacked near their stereo in full view. Songs visually connected to images on the sleeve offered some meaning, some insight into the owner. Like wearing a t-shirt or a pin from your favorite bands."

"However, it's different now. Songs are locked up in hard drives with passwords or they're spinning atoms in some vast indifferent cyberspace. I carry my music on a silly little flash drive. A puny circuit board with no character, no personality, but more data space than a small town library. I'm not saying it's better or worse. Just saying that with all the accessibility we have to music now, it's become more secretive. Hidden."

~

There's silence for a moment. I pull a record from the wall. Slide the printed cardboard sleeve from the protective plastic cover then slip the vinyl from the inner yellowed paper envelope. A twelve inch black orb emerges from hibernation. Every time I lift a record, I feel a faint heart beat in my finger. Like something throbbing inside limited space. Something new and ready to be born.

I hold it in dry palms admiring the wear and tear in the angled light. Slight scratches. Smudged fingerprints. Proof of use. Place it on the mat careful to fit the nipple in the center hole. It eases in like it's done this before.

I watch it spin at thirty-three revolutions per minute. Fast enough to blur the printed center label. Leaning closer I take the corner of my shirt and moisten it with saliva. Dip the shirt onto the stiff wax applying enough pressure to remove any surface debris. I let it spin several times caressing back and forth. The smell is overwhelmingly familiar. Undertones of an empty Romeo & Julieta cigar box mask a hint of library mildewy musk.

I lift the stylus arm from its mount careful not to abruptly jar the sensitive needle. Before placing it on the outermost edge of the spinning record, I lick my forefinger and thumb and remove a trace of lint from the needle point. I then place the needle on the record near the edge before the etched grooves begin.

The silence of a record before the music starts is like an aphrodisiac. Alarmingly short and expectant. Charged and pregnant with possibility. A tick. A skip. A hum. A whirl. A rumble.

And then the music gushes forth.

~

"It continues to amaze me what a breakthrough technology the phonograph record was. Edison invented it in the eighteen hundreds, four hundred years after the printing press. It's historical. It was the first time humans were able to share recordings of sounds."

"Before that, without an instrument to play, music was indecipherable symbols on paper that few could read. Let alone translate into sound. Secret code."

I amble towards the armchair.

"To be candid with you, since you asked, I have other appetites that I like to indulge in addition to my vinyl fetish."

"What is it that you prefer? Chains? Whips? Melted dark chocolate," she jokes.

"Well, it differs all the time. It's all harmless stuff. But more often than not, it involves an attraction to new experiences. You see, I like having sex with strangers." This I submit, aware that it may be too much.

"Every stranger is a friend you have yet to meet. Right? You must meet a lot of interesting people in your travels.

Come around here, let me see you," the voice in the armchair requests in a mocking half tone.

I slide around the groping arm of the chair. Shifting into view.

"You look like a drowned rat," she offers, glancing out from the corners of subdued eyes, thick with layered eye shadow and tarred mascara.

"You look like a crippled swan," I respond.

"I am a crippled swan," she says.

And she is. Wrapped in a mohair blanket. White as snow with the most mournful jet black eyes, her neck curling like a question mark from a hidden void. An ageless beautiful artifact or a beaten bird of paradise?

If she were a character from a book made into a movie, she would be played by Sasha Grey. No not Sasha Grey. More like Amy Winehouse. Wait, she's dead. Maybe Chan Marshall. Or Yolandie Visser. Fuck it, we've got to give this role to Hope Sandoval.

～

"**Y**ou look like you need some sleep," she suggests comfortingly.

"I don't sleep on weekends."

"Do you need some help making it through tonight?"

"Sure. What you got?"

She reaches into the void. Feathers ruffle. Clawed fingers emerge with an antique tobacco tin.

Unfurling her neck in my direction, she offers it to me with those eyes.

I take the tin and ask what's inside.

"It doesn't have a name yet. We've been testing them for a while and we're all hooked. Kind of like Vicodin or Norco with a twist. Take three. One will make you drowsy but three will perk you up. It's next generation synthetic opiate. I call it Cubic. Three times the pleasure."

I open the box and drop three cubed little pills into my palm and then onto my tongue.

"We grow them on trees."

"What do you mean?" I say.

She points to the orchard beyond the garden, and offers, "Allow me to show you something that will blow your mind."

~

I pick up the blanketed bundle which is lighter than I imagined and with her tucked under one arm, we climb through the window. Maneuvering between wedding guests and staff balancing trays of appetizers and aperitifs in the air, we cross the splendid lawn and enter an orchard with blossoming flowers in the colors of the rainbow.

"These trees are a new species. Genetically modified. They've mashed up the DNA of the poppy and the cherry tree and come up with something very unique. I'm not sure they fully grasp the consequences."

"Who is 'they'?" I ask.

"My uncle and his minions. As you may have realized, our families are quite rich and powerful. While my brother has a room full of mathematicians and programmers figuring out horse racing odds, my crazy uncle decided to go about reviving our family legacy – the opium trade. Who hasn't noticed that big pharma is the biggest growing industry in the world? Legal designer drugs are epidemic. While they're killing each other on the borders and in the streets over heroin, cocaine, and weed, opiates have been accepted in every household like some kind of adult candy.

"My uncle hired the smartest botanists and the best biologists to re-sequence the DNA of the poppy flower with other exotic compounds. He experimented with several flowering hosts and these weeping cherry trees yielded something unexpected."

"It's like the love child of Monsanto and GlaxoSmithKlein. If they only knew what we have here."

She points to the trees with their bushels of multi-colored flowers. Each tree producing a different color palette.

"Be still now. Listen to the trees." She cranes her neck, touching and tangling with mine.

In the silence, between the breeze and the wind, there is the softest of sounds. Like wind chime bells coming from every direction. Moving up and down scales like a trained pianist, though softer than humanly possible. As if the trees are playing their own song. The sounds flitter and flicker like reflections on a river. They float in and out of each other in heavenly harmony.

"The trees have a sonic vibration. You can hear it. What's incredible is that nature has continued to tweak the original genetic modification and has come up with her own variations.

There are seven of them. They flower in seven different colors. The flowers produce narcotic capsules. Within each pollen pocket there are nodules that contain a perfect dose of the active compound. Each of the seven slightly different from the other in potency and psycho effects."

I listen with eyes closed, feathers caressing my neck like a silk scarf. The sounds are perfectly in key like a diatonic scale. It's the most beautiful sound I've ever heard.

"This is our little family secret. We've been enjoying the experiment for years. There's nothing quite like it on earth."

With dusk arriving and the spring moon illuminating the orchard, it's as if an hourglass has been turned. The urge to set the blanket down and run my fingers through the blossoms in the sand overwhelms me. A fertile valley calls my name.

Nine billion tales told over time. Her skin is soft to the touch. Petals and sand beneath my toes. The way her lips unbutton and undress. The beating of wings suggests flight but she's going nowhere. Stretched limbs freed of the cage of her corset.

With the humor of inter species cross pollination circling through my mind, I'm at the fair riding with the swan on Mary Poppins' carousel. With whispering delicate melodies flittering through the air, we pin each other down and feast until there's nothing left. Not even a crumb. Bones licked. Marrow sucked dry.

A swan's mating dance is epically detailed and choreographed. Intercourse is energetic and brief. There is majesty and reverence in the post-coital dance which is like a synchronized ballet. Watch it on YouTube and you'll be impressed too.

Lying against her pillowy breast, gazing up, I notice the shape of the petals. They are cubic. Unnaturally arranged in delicate prisms filtering starlight and moonlight and pigments of the Big Bang.

There is geometry in the humming sounds and there is music in the spacing of the stars. Everything is connected.

And she laughs a swan's laugh. And there's enough laughter to fill buckets.

Kant said that there are two things that do not need to mean anything. One is sound and the other is laughter.

Awash in both, the memory of the strange previous evening seeps through in sepia tones. Hushed and patient and in no hurry.

"I've seen these flowers before."

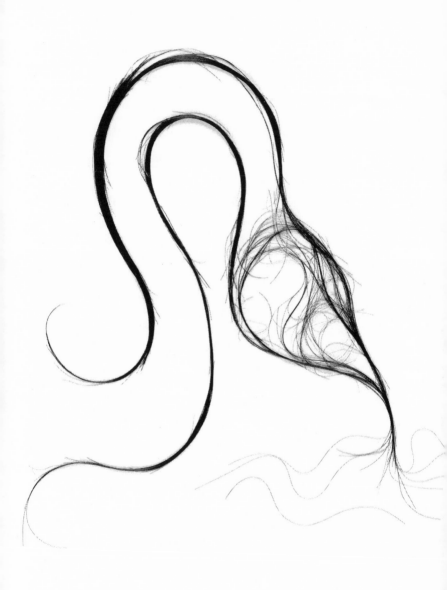

~

Everything is mysterious.

Levitating off the ground almost ten thousand Fahrenheit degrees. There are feathers everywhere. It looks like we carved a nest. Jam-packed and fortified by fornication.

Through the trees, the guests are single lining from the garden on a brick path towards dinner in the courtyard on the opposite side of the house where the ceremony took place. We can't be late so we swoop and descend unnoticed past the garden, through the window, out the basement door, into the back of the line.

The paralyzed swan is now in her wheelchair and I am guiding her. We have gravel in our voices and molting feathers speckling our clothes. Looks like we had a pillow fight and pieces of her are sticking to me. Joy in our dilated eyes like they have just seen God in high heels. It feels like a miracle inside. All sticky fingered, jellied, and bursting with flavor like leaking mochi ice cream on the beach in summertime.

Life is too short not to orgasm every day.

I'm living, truly living, like I'm going to ruin something every day. And in ruining it, I find its true essence buried inside.

Finding it right here. This is where the real shit happens. On the periphery of normalcy. Over the edge of decency. Beyond what you know. All things are possible. Who you are is limited only by who you think you are. To get past the limits of the smallness of your imagination you must only look beyond your own lashes.

I'm like a wet seed. Ready to bloom. And this is the feeling I'd like bring to the decks. But it's dinner first and I'm not hungry.

The smell of roasting pig pollutes the air. Strong noxious fumes that many people love, but I detest. Rough and arrogant like a bully punch to the nose.

~

Dinner is served family style. Each table swaddled with a complication of Chinese dishes fighting for space on a lazy Susan in the middle. A shared feast with chopsticks.

The fetid odor of burning carcass permeates the air. It gets stronger as two servants approach the altar carrying the cooked pig on a surfboard sized metal tray.

Pig flesh glazed the color of sunset. An apple in its mouth holds in place a guiltless frozen smile. The guests will feast on the sacrificial pig. Will the Gods smile down on this?

I will not. The sight disturbs me. I don't suppose the Gods would like to share in the bounty. I only hope that they are satisfied with their portion since guests are lining up to fill their plates and soon there will no meat left.

I hover behind the altar, behind the turntables, observing the gluttony with an eye for the perverse.

The woman with the clipboard appears and suggests I eat now. I politely decline telling her that I pigged out earlier on finger sandwiches. She tells me to start the music as soon as the main course dishes are cleared.

I imagine myself as the dessert. Layered chocolate and vanilla with caramel encased in a hazelnut friandise with singed marshmallow and a cherry on top. Edible petals decorating my fringes.

~

F inally, the tinkling of cutlery and crockery being removed from tables as bloated lips and cheeks parry one more bite is the signal I've been waiting for.

The music sets us free. It's come alive. And I'm a part of it. And if I align myself with it then I can steer this wedding, this moment, this experience into the sublime.

Music is magic. Invisible to the eye. A whole other spectrum. You can't touch it but it touches you. Takes you by the hand and leads you somewhere. But you've got to be open. You've got to let it in. And letting it in has nothing to do with your ears. It's a passive experience. Giving it up. Simply feeling it and being moved.

Moved to memory. Moved to joy. Hell, your feet and ass may be moved and we call that dancing. That's what DJs do.

The Cubic has opened up this little space into an arena of potential. As if someone spiked the communal wine with those naturally grown oddities from yonder that have lit me up. In spiking the wine they've bejeweled the skies.

When you're this high, the entire world is high with you. It's impossible to imagine that they're not.

They're on the dance floor. Young and old. Rattling their bones. Loose hips. In step and out of step. Jive walking. Backpedaling. Maneuvering. Jacking. Waltzing. Parading. Shimmying and shaking.

Old guys looking like they are having seizures. Old girls doing splits on the dance floor. It's spastic and fantastic. It's a commotion.

Some are frisky and some hold back. But I catch them in my net and carry them like delicate butterflies from one groove to the next. To and fro I swing from one jam to another. Tethered, captivated, and seduced they follow.

Even the tough guys with the tough jobs and the weight of empires holding them back can't resist Michael Jackson. I slink to low levels of self-worth when I'm forced to play that card. But they love it. It amazes me that the macho world folds like rice paper in the hands of an origamist when it hears the voice of that deified pedophile.

~

Using the geometry of circles, spheres, and triangles, humans have learned how to determine fixed locations of points by measurement of distance. It's a process called trilateration. Simply put, if you know the location of two co-ordinates on a plane then you can triangulate the location of the third.

This is how GPS navigation works. It's probably how birds navigate the skies across continents in flight. And it is how I am able to figure out the contingency of my situation.

I am static behind the DJ booth. A peculiar altar decorated with flowers, figurines, and other strange objects arranged to convey a subtle unspoken message. A life size sculpture of miniaturized magnificent.

The music booms like a starship on takeoff throughout the courtyard. Ricochets. Splinters. Sparks.

I play the songs that make them dance and their dancing propels me to play. All this time I watch them prance. It's a riveting point of view – the DJs perspective. Silently directing improv theater in a one seat auditorium. Manipulating an elaborate mating dance with covert questions and deceptive answers.

There are the bit players on the periphery and the leads who mingle in and off center stage. The protagonist, the bride, in the middle of the cyclone, loving the veneration. Each and every one marveling and cheering her on. Heaping praise. And as she spins closer, my heart jolts as I recognize her for the first time as the dodo-eyed mistress from the night before.

The bride in the elevator. The bride in the white room. The bride in the bloody bed.

Without a veil, those puffed, darkened, and almost extinct eyes that have seen too much of everything too soon are unforgettable. Like looking into a dark well and seeing the faintest glimmer of treasure in its distant watery depths.

Like a used record, my heart skips a beat. Sensing the beauty of danger, I wonder who else here can make this connection. Who knows that I defiled the bride on the eve of her wedding?

Those eyes catch my eyes in a resolute moment and then track over to the crippled swan in her wheelchair. The three of us aware of each other. Eyes locking and interlocking in unspoken communication. So much can be said without words. The eyes speak in silence, linking telepathically to download each other's private diaries in nanoseconds.

I triangulate that the dodo and the swan are sisters. And they have conspired to bring me here for their own benevolent reasons.

~

If I lure the bride close enough to the speaker, then I can jump into her ear. Burrow down. All she'll feel is an itch. Then slide a bit further and nuzzle. Get real comfortable and listen from her perspective.

She's moving her hips with aplomb. Like she's riding a pony. That's where she feels it. Not with her ears. Her whole body follows her hips a little behind the beat.

In her canal, tucked in like a hammock, it sounds so precise. I am hearing what she hears. She hears the whole. Like a mouthful of freshly baked meringue pie. I'm used to singling out ingredients. Hearing an egg, flour, butter, and cups of sugar. Sometimes I can tell that the eggs are newly hatched. I know if the pie was baked too long or if there were too many cooks in the kitchen.

She hears high highs and low lows. A full spectrum of frequencies. Some of them deep in the red. Slightly burned. Crisp. Subsonic and deep enough to turn me on.

Now she's feeling it too. Waves and pulses and bursts of energy. It's seismic. Eargasmic.

Let's trade places for a minute. Let her hear what I hear. It'll take some getting used to. It may take her by surprise. She might even scream. Like it's the first time. She may think it's a catastrophe. But if she relaxes. If she breathes through the difficulty then she'll realize it's an epiphany. It will be different, hearing all those individual ingredients for the first time. Hearing what the DJ hears.

I feel it tickle. She's now in my ear.

I tell her to come a little closer.

She says, "I can't come any closer. I'm locked out."

"There's good reason for that," I tell her. "I want to make sure you're ready before you go any further. Are you ready to go deeper?"

"I am. I want to see what more there is. I want to really hear what you hear. I want to get deeper inside of you," she whispers all curled up in my ear canal, toes and fingers stretching.

"I can't let you peek deep inside my brain. What if you get stuck?"

I know she won't get stuck but I'm afraid she won't like it one little bit. It's a jumble. Noisy. Messy. Like spaghetti bolognese on the kitchen floor. Discombobulated. She might get thrown into a state of confusion.

"You'll ruin that wedding dress," I tell her. "Stay where you are. Soon, you've got to get back to your guests on the dance floor."

"But please, I've never been inside a DJ's mind. It would be disappointing to be this close and not get a peek inside of yours," she pleads.

"OK," I tell her. "You asked for it, but I'm warning you, when you look inside, you'll be able to see, hear, smell everything that I do. It'll be like I'm stripped naked."

"OK. I'll open up for you now. Just a sliver."

"Holy sweet mother Jesus. What's that? It's a sickening mess. I can't quite make it out. What am I looking at?"

"You're getting a glimpse of my imagination. Everything is lewd and crude in the most abstract of ways. Past mixed with present fueled by fantasy. It's tinted in colors of my own metaphoric paradise. Ever changing. Kaleidoscopic. Oh, did you catch that? That's flesh and lace and cotton and human hair. I'm a child looking up your dress darling. Twirling you around my finger."

"You wear it tight girl. That's a compliment. Looks like you're gonna have some bruises by the end of tonight. When that dress comes off there will be flesh marks. Emblazoned by waistband ruffles and garter belt elastic. Like you've been embossed."

"The thought of the marks left on your skin turns me on."

"What's that I hear?" she asks.

"Sounds like a whip but it's only a backward snare drum. The up beat. It's what I use to mix from one record to the next. I isolate it and fade two records together on top of each other. Two songs become one."

She's already getting comfortable in here. Hearing the individual parts. I didn't expect that. Thought that she'd run away.

She begins to undress and asks me to unzip her wedding dress. Then she thrusts her breast towards my mouth. They have a skewed lateral line across the top where the strap dug in too tight.

Gavin Hardkiss

"Bite my nipple."

I playfully lick along the indented flesh towards the center of her areola. Her nipple grows from the moist attention. I bite it between by tongue and top teeth in a way that can never really hurt but might leave its own mark. It's enough to excite her and provoke her. She reaches a hand between my legs and cups my sex in her palm. She begins to knead and squeeze like a baker preparing a savory dessert.

She pulls and presses and stretches. I love the feeling of someone's hands between my legs.

My fingers reach around her back and crack open the warm split between her butt cheeks. Like a preheated oven warming up to a hotter temperature ready to cook something raw.

Suddenly the sound of a motor getting closer. We both look up to see a jet ski approaching with a bikini clad girl.

"Who's that?" asks the bride.

"Looks like my teenage babysitter from when I was thirteen. She was my first sexual experience. She liked to get naked and give me head in my bunk bed."

The bride continues to rub me. Arouse me.

I kiss her nipple again, leaving some wetness before moving over to the other one which has been patiently awaiting its turn. Tongue and teeth work the edges and I bite the flesh until it too becomes full and pointed.

Then a limousine appears and backs up into a parking space. Two girls in prom dresses exit and gaze around as if they're looking for a way in.

"Wow!" says the bride, "I thought we were on our own here. Now who's that?"

"Hah! That looks like the two girls I took to the high school prom. That was quite a memorable night. First threesome."

"What are all these other girls doing here?" the bride asks.

"Don't be jealous. It's what happens when I get intimate. This kind of excitement awakens fond memories of previous encounters. There are always moments when I think of others. Those flashes of memories are like priceless antiques that I collect."

What I don't tell her is that sometimes it's more arousing to flicker through memories, the highlight reel of sexual encounters from the past, than to focus on what's happening now.

But this is far from dull. Good thing she can't read my mind.

"Well let's get them undressed," she declares. "I'd like to be the judge of that."

Next thing I know, it's me and four more squashing body to body in close quarters. With more hands than an octopus, no one is sure who is playing with whom. It's reckless and uncoordinated but we're equally thrilled as hands make way for feet and feet make way for tongues to press their way between hair and flesh.

The feeling of my babysitter suckling between my legs while I kiss the bride is as good as it gets. Better than you can imagine.

The bride is now sitting on one of the prom girls' chest. Boobs parting to make way for slight cheeks. Her own fingers press play on her clit ring. The second prom girl positions her head near her buddy's feet as she lays herself on top, inversely pubic to pubic.

Two triangles make a star.

Looking up at me, the bride moves her lips off me to lean in to the two pussies in front of her. Like a viper, her tongue tastes various sources of nectar. Skin can taste so different from person to person. Body part to body part.

Can you taste the carnivore in her? Is that L'Oreal moisturizer or Nivea sunblock? Some trace of chlorine. A few kernels of sand. Jet ski girl came from the beach.

As the bride stretches forward her ass rises into the face of the girl she is sitting on. A tattooed lobster points its claws at the anal opening.

I gaze on from the side at the feast of flesh as the babysitter continues her solitary work below. Suckling away.

It's a gang of five. A five piece band. A five star dining experience which bursts into a chain reaction. Back to back orgasms. One sparking the other in a succession of rippled after quakes.

The bride lifts her head, hair still back in a tight bun. Turning round with a smile and juice on her chin she asks, "What's that smell? It smells kinda like rubber."

"No. That's hot Vaseline," I say as I continue to touch myself.

"I'm gonna close the door now. You've seen enough girl. Get back on the dance floor."

"Please can I stay just a little longer?" she pleads.

"This DJ still has some work to do and there are still a lot of wedding guests who want to dance with you."

"Perhaps we can continue later."

◠

I bought a one-way ticket to paradise. Problem is that I don't know when to get off.

Jean Cocteau said, "Everything one does in life, even love, occurs in an express train racing toward death. To smoke opium is to get out of the train while it is still moving."

The Cubic has a different quality to the opium. I felt like resting earlier. Now I feel like I'm racing. With no end in sight. Riding the wild tiger between the mountains through the valleys across the streams.

When the mood shifts, it can do so in a minute. You don't know why it happens but you can't get back to that moment before. It may be the witching hour. Or the wind. Or the temperature. Or the drugs. Or the song. Best not to think about it because going backwards is not an option.

It seems like we've hit that breaking point. The guests have been hooting and hollering in drunken abandonment. Dissolving in the music like sugar in tea. The dance floor has been boiling with flailing arms and loose hips for several hours. The atmosphere full of revelry until now.

Suddenly atrophy. People heading off. Some in a hurry. Doubled over. And that smell in the air is not anything like Vaseline at all. It's sour. Pungent. Rotten to the core.

I've still got to manage what's left of my dance floor. Judging that I have five minutes until the next song, I skip off to find a bathroom to pee. Heading upstairs from the courtyard, I notice something revolting. Footprints of shit on the floor. Like someone left a trail of thick brown paint and it's leading to the bathroom. There's a line of ashen faces impatiently waiting for the toilet door to open. Bent over bodies. The stench of vomit and shit is overpowering. I jump the line. Pants down, eyes closed, I feel relief. And then I notice the skid marks on the seat. What the fuck?

At this point, I get it. I realize that the Gods are playing another trick. It's a gag. The most powerful members of society, hoodlums, gangsters, Ponzi financial advisers, criminal bankers, and a bevy of benefactors of colonial oppression laid to waste by a solitary farm animal. Everyone has an atrocious case of food poisoning from eating a dirty pig.

Maybe the Gods are showing that, after all, they're not pleased with this union. Huddled around a cloud looking down on this wicked wedding, they're doubled over too. In laughter. These Gods are pranksters. They like to play tricks on mortals. Upset the table and set the balance right.

Back on my dance floor, the only ones left standing are the vegetarians, the vegans, and those vaccinated with the Cubic who were too high to eat.

～

It's one of those unfortunate things that you can spend a year planning a wedding and you never know how it's going to turn out. You hope for the best, but you're packing a lot of expectation into five hours.

It could rain. Or worse.

It's deep into the late night. The guests have made an uneasy retreat to their Rolls Royces which will shuttle them back to their own private porcelain lavatories in the sky. There they will spend an uneasy few days sweating and swearing that they were purposely poisoned. They will debate whether the groom's family or the bride's family is to blame. They will use words like vendetta and revenge. Their otherwise pleasant memories of the staged wedding ceremony, the beautiful lighting, the dazzling flower arrangements, the energetic music, the diplomatic speeches, and the fucking monogrammed table linen will be eclipsed by the image of a smiling dead pig with an apple in its mouth. An apple that fell too far from the tree.

Meanwhile those few that remain have made a placid retreat to the comfort of the basement. A halcyon sanctuary for further late night sessions.

~

The calamity has left seven people standing.

Or sitting because everyone is stretched out. Unbuckled and untied. Lounging on a mahogany daybed and a Méridienne chaise longue while I begin to DJ a more intimate selection of tunes. This is where I break out into the true eclectic sounds. Subdued and abstract. Parallel dimensions that resonate close to my heart. Songs that few have heard before but will feel for a lifetime.

In the mood that I create, hours expand and contract into weeks and seconds as the Cubic makes its rounds again. The vegans and vegetarians merge with the intoxicated. Vertical and horizontal shadow dancing. Sensual awakenings. Moments of rapture. Moments of bliss.

Wrapped up in the warmth of sound, it's a benediction that Apollo would have liked to have made the short journey from Heaven to attend. To join the chosen few isolated on this parabolic island for an infinite moment where nothing in the world exists but sweet music. Weaving between precious songs, there is intermittent laughter and incomprehensible conversation.

~

Perhaps we're elevating higher to meet Apollo in his abode. It certainly feels that way. Unlocking doors that open to stairs that climb towards the next level. Like a maze in a pyramid that winds towards the top. As we get closer to the top, the space gets narrower and the journey becomes more challenging. Unless of course, it becomes easier. And why shouldn't it?

Each consecutive song decorates a chamber with its own upholstery, wallpaper, and lighting. Some songs offer the simple charm of an empty room. Others are cluttered with old electronics bursting from bowls and vases and lamps on every surface. Some rooms have vertical gardens built on horizontal ladders, and some have mirrors on opposite walls where you can see into infinity. Others have open windows which let in fresh air.

Pay attention closely and you'll see a cathode TV screen, which was once used for playing video games, explode. Shards of glass spin like planets defying gravity. The laws of physics are broken. Inside, the transistors, wires, and tubes breathe fresh air for the first time. With light seeping in instead of projecting out, nature takes control. She crystallizes into new forms. Pollinates. A curiosity cabinet with a miniature garden grows before your eyes. Ants with antlers look for food in the shells of snails. A long legged spider spins records in a corner. It's all in technicolor. It's all in 3D. Drops of moisture drip from inside. Focus and zoom closely into a single drop and you'll see three girls dancing in rhythm to the sound of the future inside the fertile forest of their collective minds.

It's like a mash-up of Tetris and SimCity within Bruce Lee's Game of Death with a better soundtrack.

Repetitive vocal cues are like keys or codes which allow access to a deeper plane. An angelic mantra. Looping patterns. Modified tones that reshape the surroundings.

But perhaps the pyramid is upside down and we don't realize it. Instead of rising, we're digging deeper. Going down further into the underworld. And if we reach the tip at the bottom, where will we be if there's nowhere left to go?

Undermined by fragments that no longer serve us. Hindered by pointed prisms of broken glass. Blocked by useless windows that won't open. Surrounded by lonely strangers. Haunted by black ghosts.

One song can change that. Invert the pyramid so that we are rising again. Spinning to a higher consciousness.

And so it goes. These deviations of conflict and resolution help us find a center. At that center there is bliss. Once a conflict has reached the limit of our understanding, we are free to spin like a star out of control.

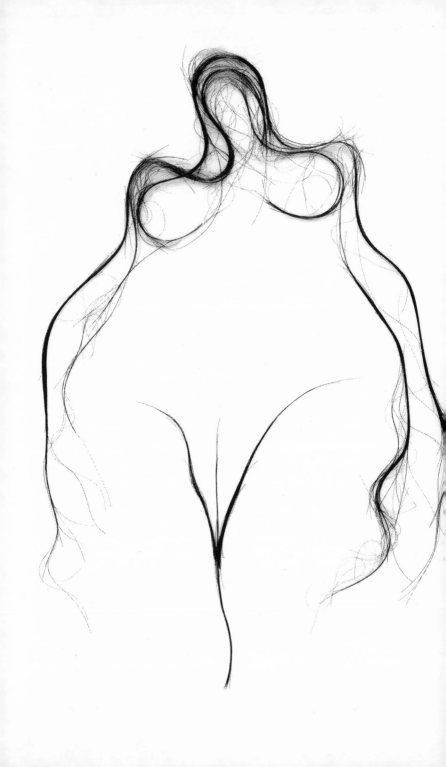

~

A kiss is like a confession.

The dodo bride and the swan corral around me, giddy and loose lipped, with arms and wings wrapped around me, they tell me that they planned it this way. Well, not the pig. That was the work of a higher order, but my involvement in this sordid affair.

They have colluded to get me. To get a piece of me. And for me to get a piece of them.

Their devious, wicked, and sinister plan to bring me to Hong Kong to have fun, notwithstanding the fallacy of the wedding, is precious. In the face of a calamitous merger of families, they found a precocious way to get the most out of the occasion. And it goes to show how truly fucked up the frayed genes of the wealthy can be. I guess everything is a business deal to the uber-rich, even having fun. And wicked girls will be wicked girls.

But there's more to it.

The Swan explains, "Our family has been living a charmed existence for generations. Wealth can buy almost everything. However, our uncle's experiment playing God with plants is something beyond what money can buy. The Cubic is a one in a million miracle. We've been living in the hyper-reality of its aura for a long time. Long enough to know that this is worth more than money can buy. There's nothing else like it. If the goal of life is to match one's heartbeat to the universe, then we've found a way."

"We're living in such an accelerated age. Old systems are failing fast. And there is this ongoing sexual revolution. We are fighting for control of our own bodies and the rules of what's permitted are for us to decide. It no longer matters how nature coded us at birth. Reproduction is a choice. Pleasure is our inalienable human right."

"My sister and I have inoculated ourselves from those outside competing realities," she says pointing away towards oblivion, "where it's difficult to tell what's real and what's fake."

"But we still have faith. Nature multiplies and bursts forth with new forms and expressions. It gives us what we need to evolve. This Cubic is still a well-kept secret but when the secret is out it could be dangerous and we fear that it might be the undoing of our family."

"Our uncle doesn't have the British Army to protect him like it protected our great grandfather."

"Running money rackets is one thing. Running revolutions is another. Having a new drug that eclipses the legal and illegal alternatives is going to make a lot of people mad as hell."

"Human society changes more abruptly than nature. What may be accepted in society at one time, may quickly become dangerous. The poppy, was once a potent respected gift of the Gods. Now it's illegal to grow. Shifting cultural attitudes and big business have changed an herbal sacrament into a poison."

"This could all go down in flames. Our uncle is a sweet-natured gardener at heart. But now he talks about burning down the orchard. He grew up in a world where you can't trust anyone. It's that post-war world view that shit is falling apart. War veterans and refugees are always running from something. It doesn't matter which war, once you've lived through one you think the worst. He's afraid that his work could fall into the wrong hands."

"That's why we need your help. To carry the weight. To bridge the generational divide. To help keep the secret. Our secret is now yours too."

"I'm honored. What can I say? I can keep a secret," I offer. "I swear I won't tell anyone."

"We choose you because we love your music and your music speaks to us in a similar way that the Cubic speaks to us. It brings a lighthearted feeling of safety and it's a connection that no one will make. There's a risk that we're taking in telling you but it feels right."

"You have my word," I say.

"There's one more thing," adds the Dodo. "We've gone to some extreme measures to protect our little secret. Dare I reveal it, but my sister and I have had the Cubic inserted into our clitoris for safekeeping. There's a vacuum sealed Cubic seed pierced into each of us."

"We thought that there can be no safer place. When we fuck it's like fucking a forest of euphoria."

And she hoists her wedding dress to reveal a familiar patch of sexuality. No underwear above the lace garter. Through her pubic hair, the flap of her petal twists sideways. She hoists the hood to reveal the barbell of her Queen Victoria into which a seed has been hermetically sealed.

I submit to the cult of the Cubic.

She pauses. Eyes half-mast.

"How's that bruise on your finger?"

I raise a limp forefinger into the light of a lamp. A shadow longer than a cat's tail is cast onto the red wallpapered wall.

"Last night, when you passed out in the white room, the nurse who was with me made an incision in your finger and inserted a wafer thin silicon chip beneath your nail with the DNA code for the Cubic."

"You're kidding me, right?" I respond dumbfounded.

"No. We're not kidding. You bled way more than expected. But it looks like it's healing fast. You can barely tell?"

"What the fuck? You've put a thumb drive in my finger? Am I hearing this right?"

"Yes. You now have the genetic code too for safekeeping. They're just zeros and ones. Might as well be a song growing inside of you. At the right time these zeros and ones can bloom into new life. You should forget about this now because it's not yet important. But the three of us hold a key to an unknown potential that we must protect. It's best for now that we forget."

Without moving her lips, she smiles with her dodo eyes.

The music bleeds into other conversations. Saturates with sonic swashes of red nail paint and colorful confetti. A stuttering voice chants over a collapsed beat. A coded message whose meaning I can't quite decipher. But in the silence of a moment before sunrise, it sounds like a mating call.

~

And the dawn cracks its yolk again. Through the half-light we are encouraging each other to greet it. Back through the windows we stumble. Together drifting with the morning mist through the dewy lawns of the garden towards the narcotic trees. Leaving the throbbing humanoid sonic tapestry behind. Music warbles into the background and the silence is golden like this sunrise.

Like zombie spirits from the catacombs of McQueen's lost collection we float. Unraveled mohair blankets trail behind erasing footprints on the ground. We're dowsing for the divine.

Within the heavenly orchard we find a spot on the highest ground from which to distill and drink this sunrise through the glistening Thebane square petals. They hover like cocoons. Pursed together until the warmth of a new day hugs them open to reveal their analgesic pearls of oxycodone, oxymorphone, nalbuphine, naloxone, naltrexone, buprenorphine, and etorphine.

Strangers become best friends at this hour. Friends for life. Cognizant of the turning of a page. Proud witnesses of the day trading places with the night. And as common as it is (for it occurs twenty-eight time more frequently than a full moon) few will stop to see the sun rise. And of those who see it, few will truly observe the wash of color striking the horizon.

Abrupt and otherworldly. Ebony phased into cobalt, ocher into primrose like a box of pastels being squashed beneath the wheels of the sun's chariot as he lifts himself up to peer over the horizon.

And of those who intensely observe it, none will see it the same.

The world spinning in oblivion. A planet in galactic motion barging down the Milky Way. There will be perfunctory views from an airplane flying above us, a ferry below us, and the trucks moving steadfastly towards rush hour destinations. Nothing quite like this with feet on the ground.

Toes cushioned by a sheet of blossoms and petals. Curling like confetti to comfort the earth.

Here. Now. Exquisite.

Good morning. We're going nowhere and we've got nowhere to be.

Nature's finest hour. Stare at the sun and you'll go blind. The mighty sun will burn a hole in your eye. But not at this hour. Eyes can stare for a breath or two longer. Gain nourishment from welcomed contact with the sun and with each other.

Eye contact held longer, long enough to notice the marvelous marbling galaxies in each other's eyes. And that's all.

Nothing more intended other than bearing witness to beauty. We're going nowhere.

Bearing interest. Barren mistress. Baron in a dress. Barometer test.

Talented people. Dilated pupils. Elated pupils.

Disassociated and abstracted, the mind wanders. Freely.

Daybreak is like the space between sleep and wakefulness. This is where dreams occur. As the night yields to the day. Within the chasm of a yawn.

Hear them. It's the trees. They are whispering to each other. A madrigal. Ancient as the wind with her fingers on her harp. Barely touching, they are whispering secrets and singing in the most ancient of languages.

Words don't do justice within the beauty of a sunrise. Share with a friend and be quiet, you'll see.

Made in the USA
San Bernardino, CA
14 August 2013